TWELVE WEEKS

TO

DEATH

Lou Parkes

This one is for Paige, for sharing my twisted interest in cults and the post-apocalypse.

ONE

Renee
Day 457
2280 C.E.

R ecording...

The rest of team Charlie are out ahead of me. They're scanning the tree line with their torchlights. The time is currently...seventeen-o-nine. We've been above ground for approximately nine minutes. Teams Alpha and Bravo split from us at checkpoint fifty-two. The sun has disappeared from view:

I

We are relying solely on our torchlights now. We're heading to checkpoint fifty-six. I'll check back in when we arrive. End of recording...'

Renee catches up to the others, careful not to trip on any tree roots as she jogs ahead. Her bag bounces on her back, the sound echoing around the otherwise quiet forest.

"Heard anything from Harriet yet?" She asks. Joey shakes his head as he continues searching the trees for any potential threat. Michaela, stuck to his other side, looks down to the roots, examining them for samples. She glances up at Renee and smiles wide, that gap-toothed grin even more ridiculous hiding under the magnifying glasses perched atop the bridge of her nose. But Renee smiles back and drifts off to other members of the group.

"How far are we from the checkpoint?" Asks David.

"Half an hour, at this rate," Aoife responds. She's looking down at the compass strapped to her wrist, pointing her torchlight right at its glass surface.

Juniper sidles up next to Renee and nudges her in the shoulder. Renee turns to look at them and raises an eyebrow. "What?" She asks.

II

Juniper's got a stupid-wide smile on their face that makes Renee suspicious of what they're about to say. "How's Isadora?"

I don't need this right now, Renee thinks to herself and rolls her eyes. She picks up her pace to move away from Juniper, but it's like there's a rubber band that only lets them get so far from one another before Juniper snaps right back to Renee's side.

"Seriously," they continue. "Mickey's been jabbering my ear off about it all day. Trouble in paradise?"

"Mickey's got no clue what he's talking about," Renee says, keeping her gaze steadily ahead, pointing the beam of her torchlight ahead of her so she can see where she's going.

Juniper scoffs. "Sure. Anyway, what do you think we'll find when we get to the checkpoint?"

"Team Echo, just like we do every other week."

"Watch out," calls Francis, from further ahead. Renee stops in her tracks and readjusts her torchlight so it captures his silhouette next to Pablo's. Juniper stops beside her, and their breath comes out loud and shaky, just like always. Every week, Renee's surprised by the fact that they don't stay behind and wait for the team to return. Every week, Juniper insists on coming with the

III

others as their second medic, even though Renee tells them, every week, that she can handle anything that happens just fine. Hardly anything ever happens anyway, so it's not like she'd need significant backup. Juniper's more helpful back at base, she says, but they never listen.

"What is it?" Joey asks, also pointing his torchlight ahead at Francis and Pablo.

"A trap." Pablo calls back. He turns to face the rest of the group, and everyone lowers their torchlights to the ground so they don't blind him.

"One of ours?" Asks Aoife.

Pablo shakes his head. "No. Be careful as you move closer." The group begins stepping carefully towards him and Francis, scanning the forest floor with their torchlights for anything suspicious, and when they meet the two men, they peer over shoulders and whisper about the trap in front of them.

On the ground ahead of them is an almost perfect rectangle of twigs and branches. None of them appear to be too heavy, and the area is covered with leaves. It's obvious that there's some kind of pit dug out beneath the arrangement, and Renee wonders whether whoever put this here is new at it. They must be, if their attempt at blending the trap into the surroundings is so bad.

"Go around," says Francis. "Be careful."

They move in a single-file line around the trap, and in retrospect, that might be where they went wrong.

A whistle sounds, loud and clear, and sharp enough to cut a slice right out of the tree in front of Renee. She and the rest of the group hold their breath, stop where they are, and scan the trees with their torchlights. Another whistle follows the first, and they start to panic.

"Cultists," says Pablo. "Go. Run!"

They dart forward, jerking ahead in a surging mass of anxiety. Ahead of Renee, someone almost immediately twists their ankle and yelps. They fall to the left, and by the time Renee realises what's happening, identifies it as David, he's already breaking through the pit's weak structure of sticks and leaves. He lets out an ear-splitting scream as he hits what Renee can only imagine are spikes a good seven or eight feet down, but she doesn't dare stop to take a look. He's gone. There's nothing she can do to help him. All she can focus on now is moving forward, surviving long enough to get word back to base so they can come back and retrieve his body. If the cultists haven't already claimed it for themselves.

Renee lurches ahead with the rest of the group, and more whistles, almost too high-pitched for their human ears to capture, sound off from all around them. The whole group splits up, moving further into the trees on their own. They've been trained for situations like this; if the cultists try to catch you, split up — it's easier to fight one of them than five.

"Renee! Wait!" She hears Juniper calling for her from behind, their laboured breathing causing them to wheeze and lag behind. Their heavy med pack rattles inside their bag. Renee's does too. But she can handle it. *This is why you should have stayed behind.* She doesn't dare look back; the roots are too large to manoeuvre without torchlight in this part of the forest, and twisting her ankle would spell certain doom. She doesn't want to end up like David, though she supposes there's still time — she's not scanning her surroundings as carefully as she should be. There could be another pit around any corner, just waiting for her to fall into.

"Renee—" Juniper calls again, but this time it's cut off by a weak inhale and a heavy thud. Renee still doesn't turn around. She doesn't need to to understand what's happened. Tears spill onto her cheeks, but she keeps pushing onward.

Whistles of different pitches and lengths continue sounding off, and Renee wonders briefly if she'll survive this ambush. If any of them will. It's a terrifying thought, and she tries to push it from her mind, but as she stumbles over branches and roots, trying to get away, she understands it's a fruitless endeavour. The cultists will kill her. This is the end of this body.

And she's right; a stabbing pain, like a knife plunged into a steak, hits her calf, and she falls to the forest floor. Agony like she's never felt before wracks her body, sends pain shooting through every nerve to her brain. She screams, and it comes out strangled and hoarse, like she hasn't spoken for weeks.

She rolls onto her back and struggles to sit up. Looking down at her calf, it's clear she won't be walking any time soon. Renee clenches her jaw and breathes hard to stop herself from screaming out again. Her gaze darts around the trees, searching for her assailant, but they're nowhere to be found.

"Come on!" She yells to nobody. "Show yourself! Coward!" A soft rustling of leaves sounds from behind her, and she spins around as quickly as she can without causing the blinding-white pain to flare up worse than it already is.

Her attacker is crouched, maybe three metres behind her, and a mask of rough brown bark is pulled down over their face. Only two small holes for the eyes tell Renee that they are even human; leaves of all colours and shades and sizes adorn the edges of their mask, and they've tilted their head so far to one side that she's surprised their neck isn't broken. A bracer on the inside of their left arm is made of a dark leather, and it's so worn down that Renee can only guess they've been hunting down her people and other innocent passersby for quite some time. Their clothes, or at least those that are visible under the breastplate made of a similar bark material as their mask, are dirty. Maybe they were once crisp and bone-white, but are now muddy and patched up with shoddy attempts at use of a needle and thread.

Adding to the inhuman nature of this being approaching Renee is their posture; there's a birdlike bearing to their mannerisms, jerking their head around as if always trying to catch some whisper on the wind. But underneath that is a feline's approach to hunting, with their fluid arm movements, and their light steps across the forest floor.

Now that they're getting closer, Renee starts to panic. Her heartrate picks up in her ears, pounding faster and harder than it ever has before. "No," she begs, her voice horrifyingly weak to her own ears. "Please, no. Please!"

But instead of firing another arrow, this time into her heart, or her brain through her eye, the attacker hesitates, and then lunges forward. They pounce on her, and she screams, and they press their fingers to her temple and push hard on the soft space behind her cheekbone until she loses consciousness.

TWO

Nell
12 Weeks
199 P.A.

T he girl lays on the table, completely still. Unmoving. Nell has seen her fair share of Bunkers in her life, but this one is by far the prettiest.

She *will be a fine addition to It's collection.*

"When should we begin the preparations?" Asks Marlowe. He hovers at the end of the table, his hands clasped in front of him, his soot-coloured robes flowing down to the floor.

Nell gives the girl a final once-over and turns to Marlowe. His choppy hair has been pushed behind his ears and away from his forehead by a cloth circlet. She hums.

"I think five days and five nights from now will please It." She smiles. "It will be delighted at what we have to give It."

Marlowe nods and turns to the table by the doorway where a collection of thin, precise knives, needles, and other tools lay, ready for use. But he does not pick one up. Instead, he stretches out his hand to the wall and presses his palm flat against the roots that have grown there. A few moments of silent concentration pass, and he turns back to Nell.

He nods once more. "It is done."

"Thank you, Marlowe." Nell says, and the unspoken command, *Leave me*, prompts his exit from the room.

Nell turns back to the girl on the table and reaches for her face. How pale, how unburdened by the sun it is. Bunkers only come to the surface at night. *Why have they not learned?* Nell wonders. The nighttime is when her people are at their strongest. The Bunkers never stand a chance.

Her skin is so soft under Nell's fingers. She retracts her hand out of fear of disturbing the girl's pristine complexion with the roughness of the calluses which have developed on her own skin. And her hair, so smooth, so shiny. Like silk, which Nell has only had the fortune of seeing twice before; this girl gets to wear it around with her every day. It is not fair.

Then there is the wound. Nell's gaze trails down the girl's body and her strange, grey clothing to her slender legs, lacking so much muscle and definition that Nell wonders how she manages to keep herself upright. Marlowe has already removed the arrow and stitched up the entry and exit points on either side of her calf. He wrapped it in cloth and elevated her leg to slow the blood loss. She will walk close to fine in a few days; by the week's end it will not matter.

THREE

Renee
Day 457
2280 C.E.

O
h, good. You are awake."

Everything's blurry when Renee prises open her eyes. The room she's in is small and dark, and she can't make out many objects or defining features. But there's a person standing right in her eyeline, and for a brief moment she wonders if she's hallucinating. Then they get closer, and she holds her breath, as if it will make herself disappear. Become invisible.

Her mouth's dry. How long has she been unconscious? She can't scream, and it wouldn't do her any good if she could. They've brought her to their camp, surely. She's surrounded by cultists.

"Hello," says the figure. A sliver of their face appears in the darkness as they step closer to Renee on the table, moonlight cutting across their features and casting odd shadows. "How are you feeling?"

Renee swallows and lets out a shaky breath. She doesn't know what to say. What she *should* say, if anything at all. Will they use what she says against her? Will they even care?

"I know you can talk," says the figure. One dark, beady eye stares, unblinking, at Renee. Their eyebrow shoots up, and the corner of their lips tugs down towards their chin. "You spoke to Emory before she brought you in."

"You mean when she shot me?" Renee can't help but say. The figure hesitates, then narrows their eye.

"Regrettably so," they say. "How are you feeling?"

Renee lets out a sigh through her nose and says, "I would be better if I hadn't been shot and brought to...wherever this is. I'd certainly be better if I wasn't tied to this table."

The figure hums. "Yes, well I was about to change that. If you will allow me," they move soundlessly to Renee's wrists, and she watches every movement as they do so. A few soft clicks later, and her wrists spring free. At once, Renee fights to sit up on the table, and reaches for the figure's throat. But they dart back before she gets there, and then they're back in the shadows. Renee can still make out the outline of their figure, though, and swings her legs around to jump up and lunge at them. Unfortunately, her legs don't comply with the thought; as soon as her right foot hits the floor, as soon as she puts weight on it, she stumbles and gasps before fully collapsing to her knees. The impact leaves both knees numb, and sends a juddering ache down her calf to the site of the wound. It takes her a moment to catch her breath, and then she looks up to the figure.

They move back into the sliver of moonlight, this time more than before, and finally, Renee catches a glimpse of their whole face. It's cast in strange shadows, but it's soft and feminine, except for the nose, which is sharp and pointed. Two eyes, hardened by the horrors they've seen, stare down at Renee. There's an odd curiosity in them, and she's taken aback by how otherworldly beautiful this person is.

"Please," Renee breathes. "Don't kill me."

"I will not," the figure shakes their head. Slowly, they reach out a hand, extended towards Renee. She hesitates, but decides if allowing herself to be pulled to her feet means survival in this moment, then she will comply. It's difficult to stand up, but she manages it with the figure's help, and sits all her weight into her uninjured leg.

"My name is Nell," says the figure, and the word comes out so naturally. Of course her name is Nell. Renee plays around with the name in her own mouth for a few moments, getting used to the way it sounds in her head. Then Nell asks, "What is your name?"

"Renee," says Renee. "Renee Clarke." Nell tilts her head and narrows her eyes.

"No," she shakes her head. "What is your real name?"

Now it's Renee's turn to narrow her eyes. Her hackles raise and her muscles tense, ready to run. Except she can't run, not now. Not yet. *How does she know that?*

"It's Renee Clarke." She says again, as if saying it enough times will make Nell believe her. She knows it won't, but she doesn't care. It's the truth.

At least, it is now.

Nell hums. "Well, if you will not tell me, that is fine. It hardly matters to me. I was simply curious." She turns, her back fully to Renee, but by the time Renee thinks to push off her foot and wrap her arms around Nell's neck, become dead weight and pull her to the ground, Nell's already too far away. When she faces Renee again, she's holding a crude imitation of a crutch, like the ones hospitals used to use when patients had injured their leg. Except this one's made of long, thick sticks and tied together by fraying ropes. She holds it out for Renee to take, and without hesitation, Renee accepts the crutch. She doesn't care if there's reciprocity expected in this gift. Right now, walking is more important than almost anything else.

"Come with me," says Nell. She goes to the door and opens it, and Renee doesn't know why she was expecting sunlight to stream through the open doorway, but it doesn't. Only pale moonlight and dim candlelight somewhere down the hall. She turns back to face Renee. "Come with me." She says again, and there's a tugging sensation somewhere in the back of Renee's mind as she adjusts her grip on the crutch and hobbles after her. The only thing worse than dying out there would be dying in here, in the dark, with no one ever knowing she was here.

XVII

At least in the hallway she has a chance of escape. Eventually.

The building is a labyrinth of hallways too wide to be a house, and doorways too short to have been an office building of any kind. As she follows Nell through the maze, Renee's thoughts wander to the next obvious option; a school. Rectangular panelling overhead decomposes, and little pieces fall to the floor, casting shadows in the candlelight on the way down. Other than that, and the occasional damp, mould, or other unidentifiable kind of stain on the flaky, white-painted brick, the hallways are relatively clean.

At last, when Renee's injured leg is beginning to feel like dead weight, Nell pushes open a door and leads her inside. Before she even enters, Renee can hear groans of pain and low murmuring voices. The light in here is much better than out in the hall, and Renee can see most details in much better clarity.

Maybe two metres from where she stands in the doorway is a floor-to-ceiling fence, made of sturdy-looking metal poles and rusty chicken wire. Behind the fence are eight people, all sitting and lying down in varying states of unconsciousness and injury. Renee recognises all of them almost immediately, and her eyes go wide upon registering what's going on.

"You've imprisoned them?" She asks Nell, who stares back at her with a blank expression that Renee can see properly for the first time. Her eyes are brown, and so is her choppy, chin-length hair.

"What did you expect?" Nell asks in return, a questioning expression behind those dark irises. "Us to be sitting around a table together and drinking tea?"

No, Renee thinks. *That would be far too human for your lot. Far too civilised.* She grinds her jaw and looks back to her friends, the group a crude amalgamation of teams Charlie and Echo.

"Open the door," says Nell, and the guard beside a padlocked section of the fence sticks a key into the lock and the fence screeches as they pull it open. Nell turns to Renee and tilts her head in the direction of the opening. "Go on," she says. "Join them."

Of course, she could run. Could turn and hobble out of here as fast as she could. But they'd catch her before she left the building, and she doesn't know her way around the halls, anyway. It'd be better to stay safe, here, for now, and wait for her leg to heal up enough to make a run for it.

So Renee grits her jaw again and hobbles over, crossing the threshold and joining the rest of her friends in the cage. The fence swings shut behind her, and she manoeuvres herself onto the floor, casting the crutch aside.

"Pablo," Renee breathes when she spots him, leaned up against the brick wall a few feet away. Harriet, Team Echo's leader, is pressing down on his thigh with both of her hands, which are covered up past the wrist in dark red blood. Renee slides over to them and assesses the damage. This is what she's been trained for. It's what she's good at.

She asks Harriet to remove her hands from Pablo's thigh, and at once, blood pours out of the wound. But Renee rolls up her sleeves and gets Harriet to take off her jacket. It's the two-toned grey they all wear, but hers are stained red. The colour seeps in all the way up to her mid-forearms. "Press this to the wound instead," Renee instructs, and Harriet obeys. "Now take it off, just for a second." She does, and Renee catches the briefest glimpse of the wound in more clarity.

An arrow pierces through Pablo's thigh. It enters from the left, but there's no sign of an exit wound. Renee purses her lips and helps Harriet apply pressure again.

She turns to the fence, where Nell still stands, watching. Burning hatred singes Renee's nerve endings, but she needs to remain calm for the sake of the rest of her group.

"Please," she says. "He needs help."

Nell shakes her head. "No," she says. "If he passes here, he will have died for a noble cause."

"Don't spout your cult bullshit to me right now," Renee spits. "Get me a needle and thread, at the very least."

"You are in no position to be making such demands," says Nell. "If you wish to treat him, you are free to do so with whatever materials you can find in there." Then, without allowing Renee the chance to respond, Nell turns and leaves the room.

"You bitch! He's going to die in here!" Renee shouts, though she knows there's no chance that her frustration will be heard out in the hall, and there's nothing that can be done about it from within this prison cell.

Harriet says, "Renee, what do we do?" Renee turns back to her and Pablo, who's barely conscious, still taking shallow breaths. Harriet shouldn't be looking to Renee for what to do; Harriet's Team Echo's leader, for fuck's sake. She should know what to do in a captive situation. But from the looks of it, Renee's the only one in here who's both had enough medical training to know what to do with Pablo and well enough to be doing anything about it.

She lets out a shaky breath and comes up with a plan. "Okay. Harriet, keep the pressure on his leg. Michaela, come over here, I need you to hold him down. Just like that, across his shoulders. Good." Renee takes in a long, deep, breath, and grasps the arrow's shaft close to Pablo's leg. On the exhale, she yanks the arrow. It barely gives way, and Pablo lets out an ear-splitting scream.

Shit. It's barbed.

"Okay," she swallows against her dry throat. "Okay, I'm sorry. Sorry. I don't know how far in it goes, but the only other option is to push it out."

"Please," Pablo begs breathlessly. He's sweating buckets, and he's trembling as he shakes his head against Renee's decision. "Please, it hurt less before you started helping. Just leave it in."

"I can't do that, Pablo." Renee shakes her head. "I either get it out and find something around here to stitch you up, — Aoife, look for thread somewhere in here, I don't care where you get it from, and a needle — or I leave it in, and you bleed out or get an infection. Those are your two options, Pablo. So, do you want to die slowly and painfully, or allow yourself a chance of survival?"

XXII

It takes Pablo a few moments to gather his thoughts, considering how much blood he must have already lost. Renee hears a scuffle somewhere behind her, but she doesn't take her eyes off Pablo as she waits for a response.

"Take it out." He says at last, his voice coming out hoarse and barely above a whisper. "Just take it out."

Renee acts fast. She readjusts her position, and lifts Pablo's injured leg. With the new leverage, and nothing in the way of where the arrow will come out, Renee instructs Michaela to continue her hold on Pablo's shoulders, and asks Harriet to help. Then, when she's got a good enough grip as possible around the shaft of the arrow, slippery and slick with Pablo's blood, Renee pushes. She holds it back at the fletches, where, when the wood meets the tough muscle in Pablo's thigh, it begins to warp. So she readjusts her grip again, this time in between the fletches and Pablo's thigh, and pushes again. Pablo screams, and tries to break from Michaela and Harriet's hold, but they manage to keep him as still as possible.

"Stop!" He yells, and his voice breaks. He bursts into tears, but Renee keeps going.

She can't see it, can't feel it, but as she continues to push the arrow deeper and deeper into Pablo's leg, Renee

XXIII

knows it's moving. She's making progress. She has to think about it as nothing more than a task to complete, otherwise she'll focus too closely on the fact that she's bringing her friend so much pain in the name of saving his life.

"We're almost there," Renee tells Pablo, though he doesn't seem to hear her, and she can't be sure that it's the truth. Someone comes up to her side, slides in between Renee and Michaela, and thrusts a tangled spool of grey thread into her line of vision.

"I unravelled it from my jacket," says Aoife, breathless. She holds out a steel needle, too, and it reflects in the light. "Managed to find this in the scraps over in the corner."

"Thanks Aoife," Renee says, but she doesn't look away from what she's doing with Pablo's leg. A few more shoves with all of her weight thrown behind them, and then the skin on the inside of Pablo's thigh begins to bulge outwards. He's still crying out and begging for her to stop, but she doesn't. She can't. She's so close to saving his life. She *won't* stop now.

One more push, Renee thinks. She takes a final deep breath and adjusts her grip on the arrow, and then watches as the arrowhead pierces Pablo's thigh from the inside out. Once the whole head is out of his leg, she moves to snap it off. It'll be easier to pull it back through the other side than to keep pushing the fletches through this way, and though some splinters might get caught inside Pablo's leg, in the meaty muscle of his thigh, it's a better alternative and will probably cause him less pain.

"Alright, Aoife, thread that needle." Renee instructs just as the arrowhead comes off the shaft. She begins pulling the arrow in the opposite direction, and it only gets caught and splinters once on the way out. After quickly wiping Pablo's blood off her hands and onto her thighs, Renee takes the needle and thread offered to her by Aoife and gets to work stitching Pablo's leg up on both sides. Her grip on the needle slips time after time, and frustration bubbles up inside her, but never does it tip the scales and outweigh the desire — no, the *need* — to get this job done. And fast.

Pablo's passed out by the time she finishes, no longer fighting against Michaela and Harriet's arms across his shoulders and chest. Renee instructs Aoife on how to check for his pulse — press the radial artery in his wrist and count how many beats per minute. He's breathing — barely. But barely is better than not at all, so Renee will count it as a win as she finally, after what feels like hours, sits back with a sigh. She has nothing to wipe the sweat from her forehead with that won't just smear blood all over her face, so Aoife offers her mostly blood-free jacket, and Renee thanks her profoundly as she takes it.

How many of them are left? As she finally checks off the mental to-do list of dealing with Pablo's leg, Renee slowly turns about the cell, scanning for familiar faces. There are eight people here. Too few. Far too few. There are — *were* — eight people in Team Charlie alone. Here, alive, there are less than that of teams Charlie and Echo combined. Renee closes her eyes and feels a single tear slip onto her cheek.

A hand sets down gently on her shoulder, and she turns to see who it is. Joey. He's not smiling. None of them are. His cheeks are tear-stained and smeared with blood. The two liquids mingle at the corners of his mouth. Renee reaches over and tries to wipe it away, but she just makes it worse, adding a third component to the miserable mixture.

"It's Jasper." Joey says. "He needs help too." Renee blinks and stops any more tears from falling as she nods and slides across the blood-soaked floor to the other side of the cell.

XXVI

There's so few people in here, but most of them need her help. Michaela has a dislocated knee from falling on it oddly in the chase; Carla's wrist is bent at an angle that it shouldn't be able to manage; Jasper has a cut from a tree branch that spans the width of his bicep and goes right to the gleaming humerus, deep in his arm.

She's up for hours, providing the medical aid to her wounded friends that they can't give themselves. By the time she's dealt with all the major injuries, everyone else has fallen asleep, and she's damn near close to it. With one hand, Renee holds the needle she's had to use on everyone without properly sterilising because there's nothing to do it with and Aoife couldn't find another in her pile of rubbish. With her other hand, she ties a knot and pulls tight on Jasper's bicep. He lets out a weak moan of protest, but he's too exhausted to do anything else, and Renee feels the same.

The moment she finishes the knot, the moment she's sure it won't give way, she checks off her final task in that mental to-do list and collapses to the floor, asleep for the first time in what feels like weeks.

FOUR

Nell
12 Weeks
199 P.A.

S he's stitched them all up." Says Marlowe, standing
in front of the desk that Nell sits behind.

Nell hums. "Good."

"Good?" Marlowe furrows his brow. "How is
that good?"

"We will have more friends to send to It at the end of
the week." Nell explains. She tucks a strand of hair behind
her ear. "This is good, Marlowe."

But Marlowe is not convinced, if his pursed lips and hesitant hum of agreement are anything to judge by.

"Have them brought food and water. I am sure with all that energy spent tending to wounds our dear new friend is exhausted. And the rest of them will need to regain their strength." Marlowe does not move to fulfil the request. "Marlowe. Now, please."

Marlowe clears his throat and stiffly bows his head. "Of course."

FIVE

Holly
457 Days
2280 C.E.

P lease, let me out. I don't want this. Not anymore.

I thought it was an honour, but you've killed me.

Please, I want to live again.

XXX

SIX

Renee
Day 458
2280 C.E.

A soft touch on her shoulder jostles Renee from her dreamless sleep. It's Harriet, with what looks like a plastic cutting board in hand. There's a small piece of dry-looking meat on it, along with less than a handful of unappealing greens. The meat looks like people have pulled pieces off of it, so Renee goes to do the same. But Harriet stops her, shakes her head.

"You have the rest of it," she says.

"But what about—"

"We've all had our share." Harriet smiles. "And besides, most of us wouldn't be alive to share it at all if it weren't for you."

Renee gives her a long look, searching for any kind of give, anything she can grab hold of and manipulate to make Harriet reconsider her offer, but there's nothing there. So she gives in and takes the chunk of meat off the cutting board. It's disgusting, and just as dry as she thought it would be. It's hard, like leather, and there's no flavour to it, but at least it's something. The greens are only marginally better, but Renee swallows them down, too. She thanks Harriet as she moves to the fence to return the cutting board to their captors.

Looking out across the battlefield of poorly-stitched wounds and blood-soaked floors, Renee feels that meat and greens begin to protest in her stomach, begin crawling its way back up her oesophagus. She swallows it back down, but the heavy, acrid stench of bile and stomach acid fills her nostrils.

She's seen devastation like this before, but never has she had to sit in the aftermath without the ability to get up and walk away, to clean her skin and sterilise her tools. Her hands are still covered in blood, so much blood she can't tell where one person's begins and another's ends. It's all cracked and flaking on her hands, and she rubs them together. Little flecks of blood fall off, like the ceiling tiles she'd noticed as she came here earlier with Nell. There's one small window up in the top corner of the room, and a little light streams through it and onto Renee's fallen friends. It's not much, but it's yellow enough to tell that it's daylight, not moonlight.

Harriet comes back over to where Renee's sitting next to Jasper, and leans against the wall beside her. "Do you have your watch?" She asks. A quick, cursory check over her wrists tells Renee that she does not, in fact, have her watch. She shakes her head. Harriet hums. "Wanted to know what time it was. I can't tell how long we've been in here."

"How did you end up here, anyway?" Renee frowns at her. "How did they get into the checkpoint?" Harriet looks down at her hands in her lap, her hair falling in front of her face. "Harriet?" Renee asks. "What happened?"

"Sierra went outside. I don't know how she got out; she shouldn't have been able to." Harriet sighs. "They got in and knocked some of us out, killed the others. Next thing I know, I wake up in here. Pablo's screaming his head off, Carla's crying in the corner. The others are still unconscious from injuries or just from being knocked out." She looks over at Renee. "Then you came in."

"Do you know what they want?" Renee asks.

"They won't say, but," Harriet swallows and looks at her hands again. She starts picking at the skin there. She doesn't need to finish her sentence. Renee knows.

They're going to kill them all.

"At least we back everything up before we leave base, right?" Harriet asks, trying to be optimistic. It doesn't help. Renee hums her agreement anyway. Plays into the false sense of hope. These bodies are never making it out of here alive.

They probably won't make it out of here at all.

The door opens and a man, probably only a year or two older than Renee, walks through into the room. He's wearing those same black robes as the sentries who've stood guard on the other side of the fence since Renee woke up. Mousy brown, unevenly cut hair falls in front of his eyes, and he smiles. His gaze lands on Renee and Harriet, still sitting against the wall in the far corner, and says, "Come with me."

The two girls look at each other, not knowing who he means. He specifies; "The one with the injured leg."

Harriet lets out a breath through her nose and passes the makeshift crutch to Renee.

"Thank you," Renee says quietly, and Harriet just nods, her eyes glazing over as she goes back to staring down at the floor in front of her. "I'll see what I can do about getting us some better supplies for stitching these guys up."

On the other side of the fence, the man says, "Follow me," and a guard opens the door for the two of them to leave.

SEVEN

Nell
12 Weeks
199 P.A.

Marlowe arrives outside with the girl who calls herself Renee and bows his head to Nell, leaving the two of them alone together.

Nell smiles. "Good morning," she says. "How are you feeling? I hear you had quite an adventurous night after I left you and your friends."

"Adventurous?" Renee repeats. She scoffs. "Yeah, you could say that. Listen, about that—"

"Come, walk with me." Nell gestures for Renee to follow. The sun has yet to reach its peak, and so, with the cover of the tall trees surrounding them, they cannot be blinded by its light or burnt by its heat. Nell begins walking, and hears the soft thump of Renee's crutch in the hard earth not far behind her.

"Is it not a lovely morning?" Nell stops and turns, waiting for Renee to catch up. She smiles at her companion, but when Renee stops hobbling along, she lets out what Nell imagines is a frustrated breath and scowls at her.

"I don't care about the fucking weather." She huffs. "Is that what you brought me out here to do? Ask me if it's a lovely morning? Because if so, I'd rather go and rot in that cell with my friends. At least then I'd be surrounded by people I actually like while I die."

"On the contrary," says Nell. She points to a collection of log seats set up around a fire, — like the old texts say people used to sit at to tell stories — and begins moving towards them. "Sit with me." Renee does so, though it looks as if the act pains her to carry out. And Nell does not think it is her leg that is aching.

"What do you know of our teachings?" Nell asks. Renee frowns, confused.

XXXVII

"Why does that matter?"

"I am sure you know something," Nell tilts her head. "Humour me."

Renee scoffs. "I didn't know you had a sense of humour," she mutters under her breath, then rolls her eyes and clears her throat. "Fine. I guess, uh, you think there's going to be another apocalypse? Is that right? That we're all going to be wiped out again?"

"In a sense," Nell nods. "It is more complicated than that, but it is a good start. We also believe that this second apocalypse, as you call it, can be — not prevented, but — postponed, for a short while, if we sacrifice that which matters most to us. We have no personal possessions, nothing that matters to us but our own lives. The only thing that matters more to us than ourselves is, well, you."

"Me?" Renee echoes, her eyebrows shooting up to her hairline in disbelief. "I matter more to you than yourself?"

"Of course." Nell says, because yes, *of course* she is. "You all are, you and your friends."

"Then why are you keeping us locked in a cell with horrifically un-sterile conditions? Why are you feeding us nothing but the scraps off your plate after you've finished your own meal? Why, if my friends and I are more important to you and your people than you are to yourselves, are you refusing to properly treat our wounds?" Renee asks. "And furthermore, why did you treat *me* and refuse to treat the others? Why me, over the rest of them?"

"Compared to the others, your bag had the most medical supplies." Nell shrugs. "We figured you were their medic, and could treat them sufficiently. So we treated you so that you could treat them."

"So you have the means to treat us yourselves, you just don't want to."

"We are not allowed to." Nell shakes her head. "Our texts bar us from providing medical aid to those we intend to save."

"But you provided medical aid to me." Renee says. "Therefore betraying your texts. You're hypocrites, is what you're saying."

Nell smiles. "No, we are not hypocrites. We do not intend to save you, Renee."

Renee frowns again. "What?" She huffs out a laugh. "I mean, not that I want to be 'saved' by you lot, but why would I be the exception to the rule?"

"We need your friends alive. You could save them, medically. We decided one life could be sacrificed so that the rest may be saved."

"And how long have you been following this scripture?"

"Near two hundred years." Nell says, and lifts her chin, proud of her people's history. Renee laughs again.

"I'm sorry, but don't you think you should change a few things two hundred years in?" She asks, a condescending smile creeping its way onto her face.

Nell tilts her head. "Do you?"

Renee's smile fades.

"If you want to talk about hypocrites, how about we talk about your people?" It is Nell's turn to smile. "You say we need to change things after almost two hundred years post-apocalypse, but will not implement changes to your own society. It really is quite genius, if you think about it. There is no need to worry about individuality when you are all the same people, generation after generation. You asked me why we decided to treat your wound and not your companions', and I told you it was because you had the most medical supplies in your backpack, but that was a lie. It was because the name 'Renee Clarke' was stitched into the bag's lining, and our Elders recognised that name

XL

from previous generations. We know that to your people, 'Renee Clarke' is a healer, a medic. A doctor, or a physician, if you want to call yourself that. So, when we brought you and your friends in, our Elders knew you could provide them medical aid, and decided that one who saves others may not be saved themselves.

"You ask for more medical supplies, but we cannot provide you with such materials. Our people are more important for our survival in this inhospitable world than yours. We will always choose to heal them, to provide them with the aid and supplies necessary to survive, and to keep them alive over your people, and expect you to do the same." Nell leans in close. Marlowe is approaching slowly from behind Renee, but she has yet to notice him. "Humans are a selfish race. We care for no one but ourselves. But we, the people who live here, who follow the scriptures, will keep the rest of our species alive."

"And how do you propose to do that?" Renee asks, her voice quiet and unsure.

"By giving It the likes of you." Says Nell. "By allowing It to feed off the dregs of humanity, satiating It's hunger. Your friends, untouched by our medical aid, will serve as an example that humans can be saved. That we can be good, and selfless, and follow a cause. But you, with your hands drenched in the blood of all that is good and right in this world, will suffer at It's hands for all eternity."

Nell leans back as Marlowe reaches them. She smiles, her grin radiating truth and warmth. "They will be sacrificed to demonstrate our worthiness, to show that we deserve to survive a little longer: You will be sacrificed because that is what you deserve. And we will continue to sacrifice Renee Clarke, to give her to It, until there are no more Renee Clarkes to give It at all."

EIGHT

Holly
458 Days
2280 C.E.

R enee? Are you there?
I don't know if you can hear me. I don't know if you care.

Please, let me out. I'm going to die in here.

I need to warn them.

NINE

Renee
Day 458
2280 C.E.

T hey come for Harriet next. And Joey. And Aoife. The only three out of the group who are conscious and haven't sustained horrendous injuries. Essentially, they can walk out of the cell on their own two feet, and for whatever reason, they're the ones being targeted.

As soon as Renee arrived back after her harrowing conversation with Nell, Harriet had jumped on her, asking what they'd talked about, wondering desperately whether they would be given anything to better treat their friends' wounds. Renee had broken the unfortunate news that no, they weren't going to be given the proper tools and supplies, and hobbled over to Pablo, set herself down by his side, and lifted up Aoife's jacket that she'd set on his leg after stitching it up.

"How's it lookin', doc?" Pablo asked weakly. His voice had come out as no more than a hoarse whisper, his vocal cords strained from all the screaming he did before he passed out. The lack of blood was surely getting to him now, too. He could barely keep his eyes awake. Pulling back the jacket, Renee almost gagged, but composed herself before any vomit spilled from her lips. The wound was yellowing with a brewing infection and the skin was puffy from where Renee had stitched it back together. The stitches were already coming apart, the thin string she'd used refusing to hold it together in Pablo's leg.

She'd been trained for years on bedside manner, how it was always best to tell your patient things were looking alright, even if they weren't, but to find a balance between false hope and the truth. She swallowed the bile in her throat and gave Pablo a watery smile. "It's the best we can hope for with what we've got." Truth. No false hope. God, she felt like a politician, and she hated it.

When they came for Harriet and the others, Renee had leaned over, grabbed her by the wrist, and said, "Don't anger them. We need to increase our chances of getting out of here as much as possible." Harriet had hesitated, nodded, and followed the woman in a black robe out the door.

Slumped beside Pablo, Renee closes her eyes and hopes for some reprieve from this nightmare, but she's faced with something almost just as bad: Memories.

Memories of the last few months before the world went to shit. These memories, one would think, with every new piece of information she gains daily, would be the first to fade. But psychological experimentations have shown that traumatic memories are some of the most potent, the ones that stick in one's mind the clearest, for the longest period of time. And though Renee wasn't personally on the surface when the bombs were dropped, she watched the news, she heard the reporters on the radio tell the public that bombs were set to be dropped globally, that everyone should head to their nearest bunker and hunker down until it was deemed safe to come back to the surface. The television had cut off, the radio had turned static, the bunker had gone eerily silent.

And the months that followed: The tireless hours working away at perfecting their experiments, at promising themselves they wouldn't turn out like the ones that had begun destroying the world and forced it to put itself out of its misery to wipe them out. And if they did end up like those experiments, they'd be the first ones — the only ones who could — to put a stop to it.

A boot softly tapping against her thigh wakes her. It's Joey. He's back. Renee sits up quickly. Too quick, in hindsight — the muscles in her calf scream in pain, and she hisses through clenched teeth.

"Are you okay?" Joey asks, crouching and reaching out to help. Renee holds up a hand as she sits upright.

"I'm fine," she says and swallows against her dry throat. "Tell me, what did they talk to you about?"

Joey sits cross-legged beside her and begins explaining. "Mostly, they wanted me to tell them what my name was. Said theirs was Marlowe." He huffs and shakes his head. "Not that that matters."

"But it might," Renee puts a hand over his where it sits on his leg and rubs it to help bring him some kind of reassurance. She smiles. "It might be useful, if we manage to get out of here. We rejoin the others — who I'm sure are already looking for Team Echo, at least, given they never made it back to base — give them the names and location of these people, and come back with everyone and their weapons in tow."

Joey nods. "I suppose. It's just hard to think about getting out of here when, well," he slouches his shoulders, and Renee looks around at the room again. She doesn't need to, though, she knows what it looks like. It's like a massacre. At least everyone's still alive. For now. An unexpected swell of pride bubbles up in her chest. If nothing else, Renee is damn good at her job.

"Anyway," Joey continues. "They also asked me a bunch of weirdly personal questions."

Renee frowns. "Personal how?"

"Like what my favourite colour is, my birthday, my favourite animal. That sort of thing. It was really weird."

That is weird. Why would these people want to get to know them if they're just going to kill them?

XLVIII

TEN

Nell
12 Weeks
199 P.A.

W hy are your people asking my friends what their favourite colour is?"

She is starting off strong this afternoon, then. Nell turns and smiles at Renee as she hobbles along beside Nell with that crutch of hers. A quick glance down at her leg tells Nell that the arrow wound is healing up nicely. There seems to be no risk of infection. She stores that away in her mind to tell Marlowe about later. Give him his credit where it is due.

"What do you know about my people's beliefs?"

"What? I thought we went over this this morning." Renee huffs.

"Yes, I suppose we did." Nell looks up at the sky. It is clear this afternoon. No clouds as far as the eye can see. It is a good day for outdoor activities. "But now I would like to know what you understand of our sacrifices."

"Just because you're keeping us in a school doesn't mean you have to treat me like a student." Renee stops walking, and Nell looks back at her. "I don't care about your fucking scriptures. They're all lies, and anyone who believes them is just as much an idiot as the person who came up with them."

"That is very rude," Nell says, warning clear in her tone. Renee narrows her eyes and throws a hand up in between them.

"Do you think I care about being rude to you right now?" She asks. "You've already told me you're going to kill me. What more do I have to lose?"

"Have you told your friends?" Nell asks. The expression on Renee's face shifts to something uncomfortable, and Nell smiles. She always loves this part; watching them squirm, like rats in a cage, desperate to avoid giving an explanation. She read something about that once. Somebody thought it would be a good idea to put a collection of hungry rats in a cage and attach it to a person's abdomen, then hold a candle to the other side of the cage and watch as the rats burrow into the person's body to escape. It is a gruesome thing to even imagine, let alone carry out. But it is fascinating to Nell, how people will act so tough until faced with the truth they have been fighting to avoid for a very long time.

"No," she says. "Of course not. You do not want to worry them, do you? It is quite heroic of you, I have to say. I wonder, are you their leader in there?" She tilts her head. "Were you their leader out here?"

Renee clenches her jaw. "I'm not a leader. Just because you decided I am doesn't make it true."

"Then who is?" Nell clasps her hands together in front of her.

"Why would I tell you that?"

"Because I think that you are lying to me, Renee. And I do not like liars."

Nell begins walking again, and it takes a few moments, but then Renee trails after her, that crutch crunching in the soft leaves again.

LI

"You have been lying to me about something since the moment you got here, in fact." Nell gives Renee a sidelong glance and a few moments for her to catch on to what she is implying. When she does, she shoots Nell an angry glare.

"My name is Renee Clarke. You seemed to know that before you even asked me, so why are you asking again?"

"Because I know how your people work. I said it earlier; it is clever. Indeed, I believe it is. But it is dehumanising, and it is the very reason you all need to be saved."

"But not me, right?" Renee asks, and there is a hint of sarcasm in her voice that has Nell on edge. Why does she resist so strongly to this fact? Every single time they speak of it, Renee seems to hate the idea that no, she cannot be saved. She is not the example of humanity that proves they are a good species, that they deserve to continue living. But it is interesting to see that, like one of those experiments Nell used to read about, no matter how many versions of Renee Clarke she meets, Renee will always remain the same. Always be steadfast in her beliefs and values. Nell almost admires that about her.

"No, Renee. Not you." Nell says. "And neither will we. None of us here, who follow the scriptures, will be saved.

We have provided you with medical aid, we have committed wrongs in order to bring your people here, to save them. They could not be saved without us, but we cannot also be saved. Do you see the point of confusion here? Our Elders certainly do."

"You mentioned these Elders earlier," Renee hobbles over to the log seats they sat at this morning. Nell joins her, but does not sit with her. "When will I get to meet them?"

"Oh, you will probably not have the pleasure," Nell shakes her head. "Not until it is your turn to join It, at least."

"Of course," Renee mutters under her breath.

Nell lets them sit in the silence for a few moments, appreciating the soft breeze and the quiet, distant chirping of birds somewhere deep in the forest. Then, she says, "What do you understand about my people's sacrifices?"

Renee lets out a long, frustrated sigh, and shrugs. "Not much, apparently. Not that I thought I'd ever need to know. Not that any of my people who you've brought here have ever made it home to tell the tale of what they saw or experienced."

"That is a fair observation." Nell says.

"Oh, is it? Is it a fair observation, Nell? Well, I'm so glad you think so, because I was really starting to worry that you didn't approve of my observations." Renee spits. She huffs a laugh, and her next words drip with sarcasm, thick like honey: "A-plus to me, I guess. For my simply stellar observations."

Nell purses her lips. "I do not appreciate your tone, Renee. I simply want to explain. I want to answer your question, the first one you asked me this afternoon."

Renee shakes her head. She throws her arms up in exasperation. "I guess it doesn't matter, does it? Fuck it, tell me, Nell. Tell me all about your sacrifices. Tell me all about your rituals."

Now she almost does not want to, but Nell clears her throat and begins.

"Our scriptures instruct us to get to know those we sacrifice for at least a week prior to saving them. Like I said this morning, the people we sacrifice — the people we *save* through sacrifice — mean infinitely more to us than we do to ourselves. In order to make sure that their sacrifice to be saved is true, and that we are not just killing without reason, our scriptures tell us that we must know them, as much as possible, before they can be saved."

LIV

Renee frowns. "That makes no fucking sense. Do you understand that? Please tell me you understand that makes no fucking sense."

Nell breathes a sigh through her nose and looks away. Never before has Renee been so angry about this fact. So hateful. Maybe it is because of how she was brought in this time. That is the only explanation Nell can think of that would justify her anger.

She walks over to a tree and bends down to inspect its roots, thick and covered in bark, just like all those surrounding it. But the roots of this tree are long, too, and extend past the log circle, past the men standing guard outside the entrance to the building, and into a room where Marlowe sits, beside the root system that has collected there over hundreds of years. Nell reaches out to touch the root, and, via her mind, sends a message down and through it, to Marlowe.

"Wait," Renee sounds scared. Nell turns her head to look at her and raises her eyebrows in a silent question, an offering to continue her train of thought.

"You're one of them?" There is a quiver in her voice, and she gets to her feet, leaning heavily on that crutch. Renee points at Nell, her shaking, outstretched finger accusatory. Nell stands up and tilts her head.

"One of whom?" Nell prompts.

Renee swallows and shakes her head, almost as if she is trying to find a way to deny this simple fact in her mind. Fascinating. Has she never responded like this before, Nell wonders, or has Renee simply never seen her send messages like this before?

"One of those mutated monsters." There is a kind of vitriol in Renee's voice that has Nell taken aback. No, she has never responded like this before. Marlowe comes running out of the building, heading straight for them. Renee hears him coming and turns around, then shoots her gaze back to Nell. "No, oh, fuck. No. Fuck!"

Renee grunts as she picks up her crutch and throws it at Nell. It hits her shoulder with a heavy thump, and Nell calls out in pain, but she does not feel anything break or crack, so she stumbles to her feet. Renee has already managed to get a few feet away, and she is making quite good distance considering her injured leg. Marlowe comes for Nell, but she shakes her head and points in Renee's direction. *We cannot let her get away.*

LVI

ELEVEN

Renee
Day 458
2280 C.E.

S he doesn't get very far. To be honest, she didn't expect to. But the thought of escaping, the slim possibility that she'd be able to get anywhere with her leg in its state, is what propelled her forward.

That, and the knowledge that going back into the school when it could be crawling with *them* is a far more terrifying prospect.

Renee trips on a tree root and falls face first into the dirt and leaves and mud of the earth. She lets out a sigh and feels tears begin to well up behind her eyes. Not from the pain of landing face first, but because she understands, now, that she is going to die. Of course, it doesn't matter, it'll be like no time has passed, and she won't even remember any of her time with these people, but in the moment, right now, it feels like the world really is ending for a second time.

"Come on," comes a voice from right behind her. It's not Nell. No, this voice is gruff, and low, and frustrated. And Renee screeches and thrashes around to throw off their attempt at grappling her.

"Stop that." The voice says, angry this time, and every muscle in Renee's body tenses up like they've never done before. Her breath comes in shallow, sharp bursts.

No. No, this isn't how she's supposed to die. On her face in the dirt, paralysed, not by fear or any physical injury that would make it make sense. But by psychological warfare that she can't fight off. It's been two hundred years, but somehow the offspring of those mutated freaks are just as strong as they were back then.

Whoever had chased her into the forest slips their hand under her and picks her up. What's strange is that

LVIII

she doesn't go stiff as a board in their arms. No, instead she's floppy, all limbs everywhere, with no control over anything but the movement of her eyes and her ability to breathe. She's deadweight in their arms, but they don't drop her. She starts hyperventilating, and her mind runs wild as it tries to come up with a way to get out of this. But there isn't. So many people found that out the hard way when they got caught by one of those freaks of nature back when the government was creating them to use as weapons. As soon as one of them catches you, you're done for.

She's brought back to the log seats, where Nell is standing, the expression on her face as serene as the sky on a cloudless day. Renee wants to jump out of this person's arms and strangle Nell, but there's nothing she can do to fight the psychic hold they have on her. There's a shallow, thin cut on Nell's bicep, and a little blood bubbles up to the surface but doesn't flow down her arm. A short spark of triumph washes over Renee, if only for a moment, at the sight of the blood, at the sight of the wound she managed to inflict.

"Come now," Nell says. "Let us get you back to your friends. I am sure they will be missing you already."

LIX

Fuck you, Renee curses Nell in her head. She can't say it out loud, can't make her vocal cords conjure up the sound, can't make her lips form the words. Whoever's carrying her walks behind Nell as they make their way back to the school building. They go inside, and down the hall. Turn the corner, and another, and a third before finally coming to the room Renee's friends are locked inside.

They stop just outside the locked door, and Nell bends down so she can look Renee in the eye as she says, "You will not get away, Renee Clarke. Not from here. So stop trying to run." If Renee could say anything, do anything, she'd spit in Nell's face and call her a monster one more time, for good measure. If she's going to die in here, the least she can do is let these people know how much she despises them.

Nell stays outside as Renee's carried in. The person carrying her goes into the cage and sets her down on the dirty, bloodstained linoleum, and locks the door once more on their way out. Before they leave the room, they turn back. "Relax," they say, and a split second later all autonomy returns to Renee. Her muscles tense and she bolts to get up. She ignores the throbbing in her calf as she stumbles to the chain fence without her crutch and grips onto the thin, cutting wire like it's a lifeline.

"Fuck you," she spits at their retreating back. "Fuck you! You're all abominations! I'll kill you all!"

LXI

TWELVE

Holly
458 Days
2280 C.E.

O h, no. This isn't good. This isn't good at all.

I need to warn Sammy. Please, let me warn Sammy. He's all I have.

Please, just let me get to him. A few seconds is all I ask, then I'll go back.

Then I'll die.

I promise.

THIRTEEN

Renee
Day 458
2280 C.E.

T he bombs fell on a Tuesday. Renee can't remember what the date was. She doesn't know what month they fell, or even what year. It's been so long. But she remembers it was a Tuesday, and she remembers why they fell at all.

Her research team had specialised in implantation of information into a person's mind, but in the building they shared with other teams there was a group of twisted individuals who wanted to implant *thoughts* and *motives* into brains. They wanted to control people, and they had the government authorisation to do it.

Everyone in Renee's team thought it was an abomination. Everyone in the other teams thought so, too, but the team who worked on the twisted idea had only one thing on their mind; domination. Everyone knew they only got the funding for their research because the government wanted to use it to take out political dissidents. Anyone who opposed their absolute control was a threat, and this was the easiest way to eliminate the need for hired assassins who might spill secrets or turn on them. And besides, there was no need to pay mindless zombies who would obey every command given to them. With that research, with that ability to control so easily, they'd be able to remove any kind of humanity a person had and replace it with two thoughts; obedience and murder.

And, to Renee's shock, to her horror, it was working. The team came out of their laboratories every day for lunch smiling a little wider than the day before, talking between themselves in whispers too loud to be an accident, about how well their experimentations were going.

LXIV

But the day came, and Renee knew it would, when it backfired. Their research blew up in their faces, and the test subjects got out.

First, they went for the team who'd been experimenting on them. They attacked them, slaughtered them in the labs where they'd been poked and prodded, pulled apart and stitched back together for who knows how long. Renee remembers thinking, absentmindedly, days later, that they deserved what they got. And she stands by that. But the rest of the world didn't deserve what *it* got.

It took twenty four hours for the government to realise what had happened, and another seventy two to decide what their next course of action would be. Renee's team had already holed up in a bunker with everything they'd need for the foreseeable future by the time the bombs dropped, but it hadn't made watching what happened on the television any easier.

"Should we keep going?" Asked Harriet when the television finally cut out, static taking over. Joey pulled the cable out of the wall. There was no use for it anymore, and the static would just get annoying after a while. Grating. A reminder of the past they could never go back to. "With our research?" Harriet looked around at their faces. The forty-strong team that had made it down to the bunker stared back, a mix of terror and unsurety of the future.

"What's the point?" David shrugged. "We're going to die down here. It doesn't matter if it's a week from now or a month from now. There's no point in our research anymore. No one will ever see what becomes of it."

Diego spoke up. "Don't be so pessimistic," he said. "Sure, maybe no one will ever see what we do, but maybe we could use it to our advantage."

Harriet frowned. "What do you mean?"

"I mean, well," Diego looked around the group, seeking approval for an idea he hadn't even fully proposed yet. "We could use it on ourselves."

"We could—fuck, Diego." Sylvia ran a hand through their hair and shook their head as if they couldn't believe what they were hearing. The tips of Diego's ears went red in embarrassment. He shrank back and tried to divert all attention away from himself.

"It's not a horrible idea," Sierra spoke up, slowly. All eyes turned from Diego to Sierra, and she lifted her chin and puffed up her chest instead of shying away from it. She shrugged as nonchalantly as she could muster, and said, "I mean, think about it. If we get those farms working, — Felix, your family were buckwheat farmers, right? You've got to remember something from your childhood — and take care of the animals, — Alma, didn't you used to work on a dairy farm after you got your bachelor's? — and take care of the place properly, maybe we can keep this going longer than David's pessimistic month." She shrugged again. "Maybe we could keep this going longer than that."

"And how is our research going to help with that?" Asked Isadora. She had her arms crossed over her chest as she sat next to Renee. Dark curls framed her worried face.

"Well," Sierra continued slowly, as if she was speaking her thoughts as they came to her, unfiltered. "If we can get it to work how we want it to, and we manage to keep alive long enough, maybe we can pass it down."

It took everyone a few moments to understand what she meant by that, and then there was an uproar. A fair few agreed with Diego and Sierra's suggestion, but the overwhelming majority argued against it.

Renee didn't know what to think. Of course, it made sense. It was maybe one of the only ways that they could keep some kind of civilisation alive without spending years, decades, even, training their offspring in what they already knew, skills they already had. But, as Mickey pointed out — "You're no fucking better than they were! That's a suggestion that puts you on par with those sadistic fucks, Sierra. I won't stand for it." — it was just another form of control.

"We don't have to be like them," argued Elliott. "We can be better. It's not about control, it's about regulation."

"Do you fucking hear yourself right now?" Mason exclaimed.

"We wouldn't have to train a future generation," said Evan. "Isn't that what we were already working towards?"

"But not like this." Matilda shook her head. "We wouldn't be giving them a choice. It would be our own children. It would be *personal*."

"It was always going to be personal, Matilda. Get that through your thick fucking head." Sylvia shot back.

It was a never-ending cycle of insults and arguments, and they were never going to come to an agreement, but after it went on for almost too long, Harriet shouted above the crowd for everyone to be quiet. She took a deep breath and pinched the bridge of her nose. Harriet was the oldest of them all, with greying brown hair that was cut straight across at her chin and curled up around her ears. Thick lines marred her brow and the corners of her eyes, and everyone looked to her as an authority figure.

"How about we just sleep on it, and have a proper discussion about it in the morning," she suggested. "We're all far too worked up right now. Everyone grab a protein bar and head to bed. We'll meet back here at ten tomorrow morning."

It wasn't over, and everybody knew that, but most of them grumbled and hurried off to their rooms to sleep off the night's argument.

Renee and Isadora hung back together. Renee put a comforting arm around Isadora's shoulders, and she leaned into Renee's side as she let out an exasperated sigh. By some miracle, they were all still alive, but they'd all lost a part of themselves when the television cut to static. They were bonded, now, forever, no longer by the simple knowledge of their research focus, but by their survival. And, looking around the room, at all the haunted faces, Renee couldn't be sure how many of them wanted to be here. Alive. She wasn't even sure if she wanted to be here. At least, she supposed, it was better than the alternative. But even that didn't seem right. Maybe, she considered, they really were no better than that cursed research team. Maybe they deserved the same fate.

Only time would tell, she supposed. Time, and a vote.

LXX

FOURTEEN

Renee
Day 458
2280 C.E.

W hat was that about?" Harriet asks, slowly approaching Renee at the fence.

Renee sighs. She turns to Harriet and whispers to her. "They're *them*." Harriet's face goes pale with recognition and her mouth drops open in fear. She shakes her head, fear taking over completely.

"No," she says. "No, that's not possible. How? *How*?"

"I don't know." Renee says. "Maybe they did the same as us."

"But *how*? How did they survive?" Harriet's searching for the same answers Renee is, the same answers she doesn't have.

"I don't know," Renee says again. "I don't know, but it doesn't matter. We have to kill them."

Harriet looks up at her then, like she can't believe what she's hearing. "What?"

"What do you mean, 'what?'" Renee frowns. "Is it not obvious? We have to get out of here."

"I agree," Harriet says. "But we can't just kill them. That would make us—"

"I don't want to hear that, Harriet." Renee snaps before she can finish her sentence. "We're not having this argument again. There are only eight of us here, not forty. We have to decide what's best for the entire group's safety, even if that means taking away their choice in the matter. They'll be thankful in the long run. We've been fighting against these assholes for how long? We need them gone if we're ever going to be safe up here again."

"We'll never be safe up here, Renee," Harriet sighs. "You have to see that. Every time we send someone up here, we know there's a chance they won't come back. I

LXXII

mean, we're scientists, for fuck's sake. We're mathematicians. We're statisticians. We know the odds aren't in our favour. They never have been, and they never will be. Sure, we're threatened by this group, but how many other groups do you think are out there, just like this one? How many other groups do you think could pose a threat to us if we managed to venture further out, claim more land and checkpoints aboveground?"

She's right, of course. Renee knows it. But that doesn't mean they can't try. It doesn't mean they can't fight for their lives. Sure, they could kill themselves right now, all eight of them, and suffer no consequences. They'd all end up right back where they came from, like nothing had ever happened. But they'd have no knowledge of this place, no information to bring back to the group. Not a single one of their people have ever survived these cultists; it's why they have so little information on them. It's infuriating that though they have the upper hand of survival — no matter how many times these people kill them, their own society will never truly suffer for long because of it — they'll never know what it's like in the cultists' home. They'll never know how they operate. They'll never know that they're *them*, those abominations that research team down the hall created.

LXXIII

Renee resents those researchers, even now; they never had to suffer the long-term consequences of their actions. Never had to sit and watch as the world exploded around them.

Renee gets close to Harriet's face. "Will you fight with me? Will you get us out of here?" She whispers. She searches Harriet's eyes for some kind of answer, some kind of decision to help get them out of here. She finds nothing.

"Not at the expense of their lives." Harriet whispers back. Renee grits her teeth and rests one hand on the back of Harriet's neck.

"Okay," she says with a nod. She smiles. Swallows. Steels herself. And then, even though she knows that when she wakes up, Harriet won't remember a single second of this experience, locked in this unsanitary cell with her friends who are rotting while they still live, Renee leans in close to Harriet's ear and whispers, "Say hello to Isadora for me."

And then she snaps Harriet's neck.

And then everyone shouts.

FIFTEEN

Nell
12 Weeks
199 P.A.

O h, dear. That will not do. That will not do at *all.*
She is standing on the safe side of the fence, the side untainted by death. Renee is standing on the other side, staring into her eyes. Past her eyes, into her soul. There is a dangerous glint to Renee's gaze, a threat Nell knows she will follow through with if she ever gets out of that cage.

"You can't just keep us all in here," Renee warns. "We'll die if you do."

"You will not die in there," Nell shakes her head. "Not if you just stay put. It will not be long now, Renee." She looks out across the grief-stricken, confused faces. Many of them are collapsed on the floor, trying not to succumb to blood loss or infection. One of them is on the floor behind Renee, her neck twisted at an impossible angle. Two people, mostly uninjured, crowd her, muttering nonsense. They look up at Renee and Nell with tears in their eyes and shock on their faces.

"We may not die in *here*, but we'll still die by your hand." Renee argues. "That's no better."

"We are saving you," Nell says. "We are *helping* you. If only you would see it."

"You're going to kill us!" Renee yells. She presses herself up against the fence. It warps under the pressure, pushing outwards, towards Nell. "You're going to fucking kill us! But not if I get to you first." She spits, and little droplets of saliva hit Nell's face, but Nell pointedly ignores them and stays where she is. Right where she is. She does not even blink in the face of Renee's rage. She has seen it before. It does not scare her anymore.

"You cannot kill me," Nell says. She smiles. "You will not kill me." And just like that, something in Renee's face shifts, and she steps back from the fence. Then she scowls and grips onto it again, and starts screaming in Nell's face. Nell keeps smiling as she steps back and away. Renee's screams follow her down the hall, all the way outside, and as she continues into the forest.

It is only when she reaches the clearing where her people mill about that she notes the absence of Renee's voice, and even then, it echoes in her mind like a stone ricocheting off the walls of a well on its way down to the bottom.

They are setting up for the banquet tomorrow night. Wooden tables line the clearing with benches on either side. Candles in little wire cradles hang off ropes tied between tree branches. A seat on the far side of the clearing has a high back and is covered in moss, ferns, and flowers. It is all shaping up perfectly. Nell smiles.

Emory walks over, a bowl of soft green moss in her hands. She bows her head to Nell, who returns the gesture, and says, "Good afternoon. How are they all holding up?"

Nell does not want to spread any worry, so she continues smiling. "Perfectly fine," she says. "We are on track for their saving in three days' time." Emory smiles and nods, and hurries off in the opposite direction.

Over by the high-backed chair, Constance is readjusting the ropes in the trees. Nell makes her way over, and upon sensing her approach, Constance turns and nods.

"Constance, would you do me a favour and fetch our medic?" Nell asks. Constance nods again and abandons her previous task. She walks swiftly out of the clearing and disappears back into the forest. Nell circles the area, checking that all the preparations are just right, and then Constance is back, Guy and Freya behind her, pulling someone along with a bag over their head. They all come right for Nell, who nods at Constance and dismisses her back to the ropes.

Guy and Freya force the medic to her knees, and Guy pulls the sack off her head. Nell tilts her head and hums.

"I have a task for you, if you are up to it, Ms Mason."

SIXTEEN

Renee
Day 458
2280 C.E.

W hat the fuck, Renee?!" Joey exclaims.

"Why did you do that?" Aoife wails.

Renee ignores them both, in part because now that she's finally stopped screaming, her voice is raw and hoarse, and also because she can't bring herself to explain.

How is she supposed to tell her friends that their choice is to either meet Harriet's fate, here and now, or wait who knows how long and die at the hands of their monstrous captors? She hasn't been able to tell them their fate so far, and she's not about to deliver the confirmation of what they've probably already been expecting since they got locked in this hellhole days ago.

"It's the better option," she says at last, her voice hoarse and the words painful to squeeze out of her throat. She doesn't turn to face them. She doesn't want them to see the defeat on her face.

Really, it is the better option. Renee doesn't know what's been stopping her from killing everyone in here these past two days. Maybe it's that little part of her brain that, despite knowing that everything will be okay, that she'll wake up never knowing this ever happened, doesn't want to die. Maybe it's that she knows there isn't anyone in the bunker who could inherit what she has to give, so the community would have to wait who knows how long before having a properly trained medic again. But they'll have a new Juniper in three months, and they're close enough to what Renee can provide, so really they're no worse off without her.

Renee finally turns to face what she's done. Harriet's there, on the ground, dead. She tries not to feel bad about it. There's a second Harriet back in the bunker. They haven't really lost their leader. But here, in this place, they have. She wasn't up to the fight. Renee's always known she wouldn't be, if it came down to it. Back then, Harriet's name would have been first on that research paper if anything ever came of it. Everyone else would have been relegated to a measly *et al.* And yet, she couldn't stomach the fact that being a leader, being first on that paper, means taking charge. Means you are the most important person in the laboratory. Means at conferences, at speeches, at press releases, you are the one people turn to to ask questions about the research. About the team. About what to do when you're trapped in a bunker at the end of the world and need to decide how you're all going to survive.

Renee had taken the decision into her own hands, and she doesn't regret it. Harriet will never know, and if things go according to plan for the cultists, then neither will Renee. Neither will any of the others trapped in here. And if they do make it out, it won't matter anyway. They'll have made it out. They won't care that Renee killed Harriet, because she'll be alive and well, waiting for them when they return home.

For now, Renee has a job to do. She has to keep them alive long enough to actually make it home, and Harriet wasn't helping. Renee drops down at Pablo's side. She puts a finger under his nose to check his breathing. It's shallow. *Not good.*

The skin around where she's stitched up his wound has taken on a distressing shade, and he's sweating, his body's attempt to stave off the infection that's setting in. Most likely, without the proper care, antibiotics he desperately needs, and clean environment he should be in, Pablo will succumb to whatever infection is plaguing him. Renee clenches her jaw as she considers this. She can't be sure how long he'll last, but by a quick estimate, she doesn't think it'll be long.

The other members of their group have been slightly luckier, though she can't figure out why. Michaela's knee, now set, hasn't been bothering her much; Carla's wrist is still ailing her, but she hasn't been using it much since Renee placed it in a makeshift splint to set it relatively straight; Jasper's arm probably won't have to come off, but he's not in a much better position than Pablo. The skin around his stitches is inflamed, but he's breathing normally, and he doesn't look quite as sick as Pablo does.

One of the cultists is back. The one who carried her back here. He's got a calm smile on his face, and Renee wants to slap it off. Better yet, if she could find a blade, however small, she's sure she could find some sick satisfaction in slicing his lips away from the rest of his face. His eyes fix on Renee, and he says, "Stay there." She freezes, against her will, and her stomach is in her throat as she fights the anxiety bubbling up and threatening to explode out of her like a bomb. Her muscles seize up, and all ability to move is stolen from her as the cultist opens the fence and beckons for the others to follow him out. Joey shoots Renee a quick look before scrambling up and following him out. Michaela goes, too, and Aoife and Carla aren't far behind. The fence is closed, and the cultist turns his gaze back on Renee.

"It does not have to be like this," he says, but of course, Renee can't respond. He smiles wider, says, "Relax," and then he's gone. Renee can't even bring herself to start screaming after him this time. She just stays where she is, collapsed against the wall beside Jasper, and closes her eyes.

SEVENTEEN

Nell
12 Weeks
199 P.A.

W e are having a feast tonight," Nell says as she sits with Renee. "I would love it if you joined us."

"Why the fuck would I do that?" Renee spits. She has set her crutch at her feet, and she is clenching and unclenching her fists atop her knees. Resisting the urge to leap over and throttle Nell, no doubt. It is not possible. Not anymore. Nell has made sure of it.

She has removed the ability to kill her in Renee's mind. The desire is still there — Nell can see it in Renee's behaviour, in what she does, what she says, and is that not deeply interesting? — but she can no longer make herself jump up and kill Nell.

"Because you are hungry," Nell says. A leaf falls onto her robe in her lap, and she brushes it off to the side. "You have eaten almost nothing the past two days. We want to give you a proper meal."

"Only if my friends can come, too."

"You know I cannot promise that, Renee," Nell smiles calmly. "But I will speak to the Elders. I will see what I can do."

"Again with the fucking Elders," Renee mutters under her breath. She runs a hand down her face, and little flecks of blood that she hasn't been able to clean off flutter down to the earth with the motion. Some other bits get stuck in Renee's eyebrows and on her cheek, and Nell wants to lean over and brush them off.

"Would you like some water?" Nell asks. Renee looks up at her with a furrowed brow.

"What?"

"To clean your hands." She points to Renee's hands where they have fallen between her thighs. "They must itch with all that blood still on them." Blood covers Renee's arms up to the elbow, and some of it even stains her face, especially her forehead, where maybe she wiped the backs of her palms after stitching up her friends. Renee looks down at her hands and clenches them into fists.

"No, thanks." She mutters, and turns away. Nell hums.

"No matter. We will be getting you cleaned up later, anyway."

"What? No, I don't want to go to your stupid feast. I don't care that you're not feeding me enough. I care that my friends are dying of infections because you refuse to treat them properly."

"I have already told you why I cannot do that, Renee." Nell shakes her head.

"Then give me the tools to do it myself." Renee shoots back. "You clearly know I'm capable."

Nell clicks her tongue. "I have told you why the Elders cannot allow that, either." Renee sighs in exasperation and shakes her head as she looks away once more.

Nell wonders, for a moment, if there is a world in which she and Renee could be friends. She has tried, before, to make friends with Renee Clarke. But after a few fruitless attempts, she had decided it was not worth it to get attached to someone who did not want the friendship Nell was offering. More importantly, it was not worth it to get attached to someone who would never come around, always refused to understand Nell's way of life, and who was destined to be sacrificed for a greater cause.

"Can I show you something?" Nell asks. She stands, and Renee frowns at her. "Come with me." It is not an order, but Renee collects her crutch and follows anyway.

There has always been a murky grey area in the things Nell can say to people. She cannot give direct orders without them being forced upon whoever she is speaking to, but she has learned that if she phrases it more as a question, if she lilts the ends of her words so people understand what she is saying as a suggestion, rather than a command, she can get away with anything that is almost an order.

They round the main building and come to the glass hut where they grow some of their crops, the more tender kind that require closer care. A guard stands at attention on each side of each corner of the rectangular building, and Nell nods to them as she and Renee approach. They nod back, and Nell gestures for Renee to enter first. Renee hesitates.

"Is this where you're going to kill me?"

"If it were, I would not be bringing you here just yet." Nell replies. They stare each other down for a few moments before Renee relents and enters the hut. It is hot inside, despite the mild temperature outside. The glass traps the heat, and helps the plants grow tall and fruitful. Three rows, one on either long side of the hut, and one in the middle, line the room, and someone hums softly at the back, out of view. Renee turns back to Nell with a frown, and Nell says nothing in response. She only tilts her head, encouraging Renee onward.

They continue to the end of the row, and then Renee turns to finally see who is humming, whose voice has been echoing throughout the hut. Nell cannot see who Renee sees, but she knows who is there. And when Renee's eyes go wide and her jaw drops, Nell smiles.

"Renee?" Says Renee, trepidation dripping in the single word.

"Hmm? Oh—Holly?"

EIGHTEEN

Holly
459 Days
2280 C.E.

M^{om?}

Mom?

NINETEEN

Renee
Day 459
2280 C.E.

I t's a weird, twisted mirror that she's looking into.
Except it's not, because this woman she's looking at
is at least twenty, maybe thirty years older than
Renee is.

Renee knows who this is, of course, but the last time
she saw her was maybe five years ago. It's a confusing
thing, a genealogical dilemma. This woman, who's staring
back at her, calling her by a name that's not hers, is both

her daughter and her mother, and also an ancestor and descendant so far removed that Renee doesn't even know how many generations are between them anymore.

She is also, of course, her. She's Renee. She is both Renee and not Renee, just like Renee is both Renee and not Renee.

"I thought you were dead," Renee says, awestruck by the fact that she's alive. The older woman — herself, her daughter, her mother, her ancestor, her descendant — stands from the wooden table she sits by. The table is covered in plants and soil and ceramic planters in varying stages of brokenness, but she ignores them all in favour of stepping closer to Renee.

"How old are you now?" Older-Renee asks. The lines around her brows and on her forehead crease as she frowns in thought. "Older than eighteen, surely."

"Yes," Renee nods. Older-Renee hums and sits back down.

"So you aren't Holly anymore." She says it like a statement, but Renee swallows and shakes her head anyway. "Well, I suppose I should treat you as an intellectual equal, then. Not as a daughter."

"If you would," Renee says quietly. Something in the back of her mind flares up and she winces. It's a kind of pain she's never felt before. Or at least, a pain she's not conscious of having felt before.

Renee's only half-aware that Nell is still here, still standing no more than two metres away from her. But somehow, even though she's fought to keep her name from before a secret so far, she doesn't care. It seems to not matter anymore. Surely this Renee Clarke has already spilled the secrets, and Nell has just been playing with her the past few days. It's a twisted game she never knew she was playing, and it makes Renee want to reach over and choke her unconscious, even if she won't be able to bring herself to kill her.

"What are you doing here?" She asks older-Renee. The silent *alive* goes unsaid, but it clearly registers for her. Renee can see it in her eyes as she blinks and looks away.

"I was offered a choice, and I accepted it." Older-Renee explains. "Nell offered me a chance to stay, to live here under the care of her community, in exchange for my medical services."

Nell offered. *Her* community. Renee frowns. What about the illustrious Elders Nell keeps praising? "But they have that whole 'can't give medical aid or you'll go to Hell' thing going on."

"That only applies to outsiders, Holly," Nell pipes up. Renee turns on her and points a blood-stained finger in her face.

"Do *not* call me that. That is *not* my name." She spits. It's hard enough keeping her mind separate from the body she's in. She doesn't need Nell complicating things even further. Nell only blinks. Says nothing. Renee grinds her teeth and turns back to older-Renee.

"Why did you accept that offer?" She demands. She never would have let them keep her here against her will. If she weren't so incapacitated by her leg injury, she'd be halfway to home by now. Damn the others; any information she can bring back to the bunker is far more valuable than their lives. Their bodies are expendable, after all. Critical information that could help them figure out a way to exterminate these monsters takes precedent, every time.

Renee's not a coward. She'd kill anyone who threatened her friends. So seeing this older version of herself, who's been here at least five years, sitting in a fucking greenhouse, repotting plants and stitching up the enemy, has her enraged.

XCIII

"How long did it take them to wear you down?" She adds when older-Renee doesn't answer her question. "Did they fuck with your head?"

"No, Renee," says older-Renee. "They didn't fuck with my head. They didn't have to wear me down, because I readily accepted the offer when it was presented to me."

Renee's already-furrowed brow deepens, confusion and shock taking over completely. "Why the fuck would you accept something like that? Didn't you want to get home?"

Older-Renee sighs. "I was tired. I didn't want to keep living the way we were anymore."

"So why didn't those feelings get transferred to me?" Renee asks. None of this makes sense, but especially that part: Everybody in the bunker backs up their mind daily, and those who go above ground take particular precedence. There's no way this older version of her could have evaded backup.

"I got Isadora to falsify the information." She looks down, ashamed of what she did. At least she has the decency for that. Renee's stunned into silence. Her jaw drops open.

"I would never—"

"No," older-Renee shakes her head. "You wouldn't. *You* wouldn't. But I would."

So. Everything she's known about herself, everything she uploaded into the brain of this body when she took it over a little more than a year ago, has been a lie. At least, most things are. But how can she decide, now, what's real and what's fake? What memories are true, and what memories are fabricated by this selfish, faulty version of herself? Renee looks down at her hands, and she doesn't recognise them. She should. They've been hers for over a year now. But something in the back of her mind pokes at her consciousness, desperate to force her to remember what she used to look like. What she *really* looks like. Because this isn't her body, and this isn't her mother in front of her. It's not her daughter, not her granddaughter. Not even her great granddaughter. She can't remember how far removed she really is from the woman in front of her and the body she's in.

Her head hurts again, and this time it's a stabbing, desperate needle right behind her eye. She can't ignore it, and presses the heel of one of her palms into her browbone. Never mind that little red flakes of blood get stuck in her lashes and cloud her vision for a moment.

XCV

Never mind that someone's saying her name now — *her* name, not her body's name.

She has to get away. She has to get back to the bunker, let Harriet know what's happened, that this older-Renee is still alive, that she betrayed them, that she's not even sure if she's real anymore. It's a horrifying thought to have, but it crosses her mind and sticks somewhere right by her ear, whispering it to the cacophony of thoughts in her mind, but standing out above everything else because of its importance. Its significance.

Renee once vowed, as did the rest of the team, — or at least, she thinks she once vowed — that if things with their research ever went wrong, if things looked like they would ever take a turn to what they'd seen firsthand destroy the world, they would take care of it themselves. They would wipe themselves out. They wouldn't let themselves become the monsters they had seen wipe out everyone else.

She wants to grab one of the little spades laying on older-Renee's gardening table and shove it into her own eye cavity, pop it right out. Maybe the other one, too. Maybe then this pain in her head would stop. It would certainly fix the issue of being at the complete mercy of

XCVI

these monsters for any longer. Maybe she should grab the shears, instead, and take the sharp blades to her throat. The jugular bleeds. A lot. It would be much quicker than taking out her eyes, and would almost guarantee her death, as long as she actually hits the jugular.

But then the thought crosses her mind that she needs to get back to the bunker before she kills herself, because otherwise they'll just put her right back into someone else — who would it be? Evan's got a daughter. They can wait till she's eighteen and start the cycle all over again. No. She needs to stop this, now.

It's like any good experiment; there are variables, and a good number of them are controlled. Even. The same every time. The memories each new version of someone in the bunker gets should be a controlled variable. Not the exact same as the one that came before, maybe, but a direct and accurate continuation of what the one who came before experienced and did. Anyone who got the memories after Renee would be a variant. An uncontrolled variable. Any data they gather, anything they experience or do or say would be inaccurate and therefore of no value to the experiment.

She needs to stop this. *Now.*

"Holly, are you—"

"Don't fucking call me that!" Renee yells. She swings her arm out to whoever's stupid enough to come near her, and when her fist connects with something hard but fleshy, she rounds on them and starts hitting them. She's lost herself to a blind rage, unable to control her actions. All she can think about is getting the fuck out of this cult and back to the bunker so she can shut down the Renee tree of their experiment, even though it'll mean her permanent death.

"Stop that!" Someone yells, but it's not Nell. She's not using her fucked up freakish ability to control other people's minds. It's the older version of herself, demanding that she get off Nell, stop hitting her hard across the face. Nell hasn't said anything, hasn't forced her to stop, so she won't. Not until the very second she physically can't keep going anymore. Not until Nell's on the brink of death. And neither version of Renee will be around to nurse her back to health. She'll get her beaten and bloodied and let the lack of medical aid do the rest of the work for her.

Then there are arms around her, pulling her off Nell, and Renee screams, she kicks, she fights tooth and nail to be let go. But whoever's grabbed her — older Renee, one of the guards from outside, it doesn't matter — won't let go, despite all her protests. They pull her away, out of the greenhouse, back to the school. They don't give her any orders, though, and so she keeps fighting the whole way. Right before they carry her into the school, Renee lets herself go completely floppy all over and becomes deadweight for the person carrying her. Not expecting such a sudden change, they drop her, and she kicks out with her uninjured leg. She gets them right in the middle of their shin, and they double over, wailing and cursing in pain. With the top of their head in the perfect place, Renee kicks out again and the sole of her heavy boot lands right on the crown of their head.

She struggles to her feet and begins hobbling away, towards the tree line. Her injured leg screams at her, the muscle begging for her to stop putting so much weight on it, but she doesn't stop. She has to keep going. It takes a few hobbled steps to work up to a run, and then she's going, fast, through the tree line. People call out to her, but she doesn't stop. Blood rushes in her ears, her leg goes numb, but she keeps going.

The forest is a maze. She doesn't know where she's going, of course, but she hopes things will start looking familiar. Maybe she'll come across a checkpoint and duck inside. Maybe, if anybody's gone above ground to look for teams Charlie and Echo, she'll run into them. Maybe they'll come back with her and save everyone before leading her back home so she can terminate her data and kill herself.

She can hear voices behind her, still calling for her to stop, to come back, but none of the people are giving orders. None of them have that fucked up mutation in their DNA. She can't afford to turn around and look back. Can't risk tripping over a tree root or running into a too-low branch. If they catch up to her, she'll deal with it then, but until and unless that happens, she just has to keep on moving.

Then there's the whistles. When she starts hearing them, she knows she's in trouble. She's entered the cultists' hunting territory. And that's both the best and worst place to be, because it means she's no more than fifteen minutes from home — in which direction, though, she can't be sure — but it also means they'll almost certainly catch her. Renee takes a deep breath, picks a new direction, — left — and keeps running. The whistles keep coming, loud and sharp, some short, some long. They've never been able to figure out, for sure, what each whistle means, but Evan thinks it might be some kind of morse code. There's no time to stop to listen and work it

C

out now, though, only to run away from the sounds up in the trees and keep weaving between trunks so they can never get a clear shot on her. She doesn't know if it's working, but no arrows have hit her yet, so a tiny seed of hope begins to bloom deep in her chest.

Of course, that's the moment everything goes wrong.

They don't shoot her this time, but someone — from the trees, from behind her, she doesn't know — yells, "Stop right there!" and she freezes to the spot. She's breathless from her sprint, and looks around frantically for whoever called out to her. They don't come into view for another few long, gruelling moments, and then they're right in front of her. It's that man from before, the one who stopped her from running last time. She got significantly further this time around, though, and though that seed of hope has withered and died, a seed of pride takes its place, and its growing strong and sturdy in her heart.

He sneers at her, his chest rising and falling with each exaggerated breath in and out. She's proud of that, too, that she made him work for something he got so easily last time.

"You little bitch," he says, and Renee's taken aback. She didn't know these people even knew *how* to swear. "You'll be sorry for what you did."

She just scowls at him, since she can't give a verbal response. But then he says, "What do you have to say for yourself? Speak," and she opens her mouth and spits in his face.

"Fuck you," she says. "Fuck you and your fucking cult. You can all go to hell for all I care." He grits his jaw and slowly wipes the spit off his cheek. Then he draws back his arm, and Renee only spots the glint of the knife in his hand as he brings it down and hits her in the temple with it, knocking her unconscious.

TWENTY

Nell
12 Weeks
199 P.A.

H ow are you feeling?" Marlowe takes up position beside her. He dips a cloth into a bucket of water beside the bed and gently wipes away the blood on her face with it. Nell's cheek is so swollen it forces her left eye half-closed, and her lip is split from where Renee's knuckles made contact. The taste of blood coats her throat in a thick, mucus-like layer. It hurts like a million tonnes of soil have been pressed onto the side of her face when she moves her eyes across to look at Marlowe.

"I am fine," she manages to choke out against that blanket of blood in her throat. "I will be ready for the feast tonight."

"Nell, I don't think—"

"I will be ready for the feast tonight." She says again, this time with as much power and finality in her voice as she can muster up. It is like she is trying to convince herself, as she does with other people, to do something. If she says it enough times, maybe she will gather up the strength to make it come true.

Marlowe purses his lips but does not say anything else. Does not push her decision, though it is clear he wants to. They lapse into silence, and Nell is thankful for it; the sound of their voices had a headache blooming behind her eyes, and it dies down in the absence of the droning sound.

She wonders, as she lays there, pain lancing up and down her body, Marlowe carefully dabbing away at the blood smeared across her cheeks, what it was that finally sent Renee — *Holly*, she has to remind herself, that is her *real* name — over the edge. She would not have been able to kill Nell, even if there was not anyone else around to pull her off, to stop her attack, but the fact that she was willing to try anyway, despite the block in her mind, intrigues Nell to no end. The headache is back full force as she begins thinking on this, but she does not mind. Addison — Holly's mother, the Renee who has lived here, with Nell and her people, for five years now — stitched up a nasty cut that Holly's knuckles left on Nell's temple, and now the area emanates a dull ache. She cannot bring herself to care much about the feeling, though, nor the headache, because they do not matter. They have never mattered, in the long run. The only thing that does matter is Holly's friends and their sacrifice at the week's end. Their sacrifice will buy another few years, surely.

The risk with this belief is, of course, that they will not know until the prophesised true-collapse of civilisation arrives and passes. The people here live in a constant state of fear that their actions will not have been enough, that the end of civilisation will come and be true, rather than postponed due to the sacrifice of those they hold dear. But Nell has never really worried, because she knows, at the very least, that her conviction is enough to buy them some time, even if no one else's burns quite as strong as her own.

"Where is Holly?" Nell rasps. Marlowe tilts his head in question. "Renee," she clarifies, because Marlowe does not know her real name, and his expression clears, only to turn dark, a storm cloud swirling in his slate-grey eyes.

"Unconscious, but back in our care. She tried to run." He explains. Nell tries to hum, but the sound gets caught in her blood-slicked throat, and comes out a garbled mess, sounding more like someone being drowned desperate for air than anything else.

"Have her readied for the feast." Nell instructs. Marlowe scowls and goes to argue, but Nell raises a slow, shaky hand and he stops. "She is important for this, Marlowe. You know that. You cannot avoid that truth just because you do not like her."

Marlowe grits his jaw and looks away from her face. He clutches the cloth tightly in his fist and the water that soaks it through squeezes out and drips back into the bucket by his feet. Nell frowns softly, just enough to feel the headache behind her eyes again, and ever-so-slightly turns her head to get a better look at him.

"Marlowe?" Nell asks, the word phlegmy and distant-sounding, but he hears her all the same. She knows he does, because his eye twitches, and there's something in that expression she does not think she has ever seen in him before. Guilt? Shame? She cannot make it out, but says, "Marlowe, look at me," and he has no other choice but to turn his head and look her in the eye. The room is dimly lit, with only a few candles spread unevenly around, and the firelight flickers in Marlowe's eyes as he stares back at her. That emotion she could not name if she tried changes in a split second, becomes determination, and Nell is even more confused by that change.

"Marlowe, tell me what you are thinking." She hates to use her words on her people like this — *especially* Marlowe — but she needs to know.

He tries to fight it, and succeeds for all of two seconds before he opens his mouth and says, "It's not right."

"What is not right, Marlowe?"

"What we do to them. What the scriptures ask of us. It's not fair." He swallows and frowns deeper. "They tell us to get closer to these people we save, only to kill them at the end. It's not fair on our psyche, and it's not fair to ask that of us."

Nell has questioned, for some time now, the strength of Marlowe's conviction in their cause. He has always been her most trusted confidante, but lately that trust has begun wavering. It started with the last batch of

Bunkers they saved, when he got, in Nell's opinion, *too* close to one of them. She had not thought it possible for them to get too close to those they intend to save, but when Marlowe became uncooperative and uncommunicative for weeks after their saving, rather than the mere days most everyone else took to recoup, Nell started considering whether it is possible, after all.

"We do not kill them," she says, raising her shaky hand to Marlowe's cheek. There is still slick blood on her fingertips, and she drags them down the side of his face, smearing the crimson-coloured paint across his skin. Four lines trail down his cheek, but he does not move to wipe them away. Does not even look away from Nell's eyes as she does this to his face. "We save them, Marlowe. We *save* them, in a way that we cannot be saved ourselves."

He swallows. "But do we deserve to continue living with no promise of salvation when it's all over? Do they deserve to stop living in order to be saved? It's unfair, unbalanced, and I don't agree with it." He finally looks away and whispers, "Not anymore."

Nell says, "You cannot be saved."

Marlowe says, "I know."

Then you will die.

CVIII

TWENTY ONE

Holly
459 Days
2280 C.E.

G ive me my life back, Renee. I want my life back.

It was never yours to take.

Let me speak to my mother, if you cannot get me home to speak to my brother.

Let me out, Renee. If I'm going to die, I at least want to be in control of my body when I go.

TWENTY TWO

Day 1
2280 C.E.

W hen she comes to, she's sitting in a chair, and there are unfamiliar weights in her hands, which are stretched out in front of her. Something is pressed to each of her forearms, and when she finally opens her eyes, she sees that two of the cultists are holding her arms out and pressing wet cloths to her arms, gently cleaning off the blood there. She goes to yank her arms out of their grip, but someone says, "Stop," and she does. The cultists continue their work, and she looks up at the person who spoke. It's not the man she's used to seeing, who she's used to telling her what to do. But it is a familiar face. It comes to her quickly, where she's seen this woman before; the forest. She's the one who shot her through the calf. There is the same birdlike jerkiness to the way she moves her head. What did Nell call her? Emory?

Emory doesn't say anything else. She just stands in the corner of the room, her hands clasped behind her, a silent watcher to the cleaning in front of her. Once the cultists are satisfied that her arms are clean, they drop their cloths back into their buckets and set them aside. One of them leaves the room and comes back in a moment later, carrying a dress. It's stunning, and almost perfectly-kept, despite the world it's been forced to exist in. Near-white fabric drapes shapely and reaches the floor from where the cultist holds it at their shoulder-height. A shining strip of tiny gemstones, more likely stuck-on diamantes than real, expensive diamonds, follows the top hemline, with only five or six empty patches. It's a miracle it's kept so well for two hundred years, but she suspects they only bring it out for special occasions.

CXI

She wants to fight this, wants to lash out and scream that she won't let them put her in such a beautiful garment to kill her, but she can't. She can't move, can't speak. It's a full-body paralysis Emory has submitted her to, and she hates every second of it.

"Comply," says Emory, and the cultists with the dress manoeuvre her into such a position that allows them to pull her clothes off her and slip the dress on over her bra and underwear. She helps them only because she's forced to, and she glares daggers into the crowns of their head every time they readjust her limbs and position her just so. She feels like a marionette doll, only they have the saving grace of not being sentient. She's afforded no such liberties, and the cultists' roving, searching hands sends bile up her oesophagus in seconds.

Once it's finally on, and they've done up the buttons at her back, the cultists shuffle out of the room. Emory steps closer and gives her a once-over. This close, she can see the four crimson lines streaking down one of Emory's cheeks, and a terrifying thought crosses her mind — *who did they kill?* — as she realises she can't tell how fresh the blood looks. She makes a mental list of everyone she left behind in the cage this morning, and can't decide who would have been so stupid to have pissed one of these people off so badly that they'd kill them. After too many seconds, Emory nods, satisfied, and instructs her to follow her out of the room. With no other choice, she goes, like a dog on a leash, following a few steps behind Emory, but never straying from the path through the hallways.

It's dark when they make it outside, and she looks around, breathing in the fresh air. Emory doesn't stop here, though, and she's only half-aware that she's probably being led to her death. In this moment, looking out across the clearing in front of the building, it doesn't seem to matter that she won't make it home. It's a fleeting thought, but it crosses her mind nonetheless, and she winces as she tries to repress the idea of never making it back to the bunker. She pushes the thought away in favour of hope that she'll somehow get out of this. It's a small seed, settled somewhere atop her diaphragm, between her ribs, but it exists despite everything.

Emory leads her through the woods to a clearing where string lights have been wrapped around tree branches and wooden tables have been set up in a circle around the clearing. All the seats are filled by cultists dressed head-to-toe in black robes, and each and every one of them has those four red lines down one cheek. On the opposite side of the clearing, sitting in a high-backed chair, half-rotted with time and bitten to pieces by hungry mites' who'd gotten a hold of it, is Nell. Nell's dressed in regalia similar to her own, only its fabric is black, and the diamantes that glimmer across her clavicle are a deep ruby red that she's half-convinced are a result of almost two-hundred years of blood sacrifice.

And perhaps most disturbing of all is not the fact that Nell has positioned herself so that she appears as some sort of benevolent ruler, it is not the fact that all the cultists are staring at her as if she is nothing but an animal on show: It is that behind Nell, strung up between two trees, is Elias, his arms and legs spread out like he's some kind of star. All of his clothes have been removed, and there are gaping holes in his flesh, spread out evenly and with his guts spilling out of his torso. Flaps of skin droop down from his arms, and his entire body has become so pale and translucent that if she were not certain that he's dead, she would worry about his health.

Her breath catches — what have they done to Elias? Why have they brought him here? She looks around at the cultists, sees empty plates. But didn't Nell say this would be a feast?

"Welcome," Nell says. She extends her arms from her position in that high-backed chair as Emory leads her to the centre of the circle and forces her to her knees. They ache where she slams them into the dirt, but the only way anyone would be able to tell it pains her is the slight wince on her face and the sharp breath she sucks in through her teeth.

"Tonight, we celebrate those we will save. In two days and two nights' time, their painful existences on this planet will come to an end, and their forever-happiness will begin. To represent the Bunkers we will save, I present Holly Mason." Nell turns one outstretched arm down to her where she kneels in the middle of the clearing. Emory has disappeared from behind her, and she is all alone, surrounded by these monstrous cultists. It is almost imperceptible in the darkness, but Nell's brows draw together ever-so-slightly, and she tilts her head and considers her as she kneels before Nell. What Nell's looking for, she doesn't know, and she can't tell if she finds it, either. She doesn't care either way, she only cares about the high-pitched screeching that follows Nell's declaration.

The cultists throw back their heads and begin an unholy chorus of screams. Wolves' resonant howls; birds' insistent squawks; foxes' piercing screeches. Each of them somehow more destructive to her eardrums than the last. But she doesn't bring her hands up to protect her ears. She can't. So she settles for squeezing her eyes tight and dipping her chin to her chest as if it'll help at all.

It doesn't really, but it does manage to muffle the screams somewhat, and then, just as suddenly as they had begun, they stop. When she opens her eyes, she's startled into complete stillness. She stops breathing, she stops thinking. All she can see is Nell's doe-like eyes staring deep into her soul, right in front of her. Nell's so close she can feel her hot breath on her face.

"You are Holly," Nell whispers. The echoes of the screams have died out, and these two words are what she focuses on as she stares right back at Nell. She could shake her head, could try to convince Nell that no, she's not Holly. But what use would lying do for her now?

She nods.

Nell smiles.

TWENTY THREE

Renee
1 Day
2280 C.E.

H olly. What the fuck have you done? Holly, give me control. Let me out.

Holly. Come on, don't be stupid. That was always Sammy's thing, not yours.

I can save you, but only if you let me.

HOLLY. LET ME THE FUCK OUT. SHE'LL KILL YOU IF YOU DON'T.

TWENTY FOUR

Nell
12 Weeks
199 P.A.

H olly stares up at Nell, and it is like the world stops spinning. Fear is the most present emotion in Holly's eyes, but mixed in with that is curiosity, and maybe something like happiness. Not quite joy, but a quickly, quietly calculated safety that Holly believes Nell will extend to her.

This is unexpected. Nell did not know it was possible for the original soul in a Bunker's body to resurface. It has not happened with Addison, and for it to occur with her daughter, with Holly and with Renee, is astounding. The most headstrong opposition to Nell's community. And all it took was Holly seeing her mother for it to happen. It is almost sentimental, almost a lovely thought. But Nell knows better. Surely it was not the sentimentality of seeing her mother again that brought Holly back to the surface; rather, it was a desperation to plead her case with Nell, to beg for freedom, or perhaps forgiveness.

Nell does not care. She will not afford Holly either, and she will not save her, because it is not Renee's soul that could not be saved; it is the entire body. Humans are multicellular organisms, and like any community who have all taken part in committing a crime, the whole entity is to be treated equally. One individual cannot be to blame for the entire group's actions, and the same goes for a Bunker like Holly. She may not have been in control of her faculties while Renee had clung onto her like a parasite, but her body was complicit, and so it is the body's actions which are being punished when Nell refuses to save it, rather than the soul in charge at the time. The blood is on the hands, after all, not only the conscience.

"I cannot stop this," Nell says, quietly, to Holly. Holly swallows and blinks up at her, and that hope for safety is shuttered away behind overwhelming fear. For her life. For her friends' lives. For what happens next.

"Please," Holly's voice breaks as she all but breathes her desperation. It washes over Nell like a wave upon a rock, and slinks back off to the sea, not a threat to her resolve. "I'll do anything. *Anything.*"

Why is she so desperate to live, Nell wonders. She has come to expect this behaviour, this way of thinking, from Renee, the parasitic memory in Holly's head, but now she wonders if this overwhelming eagerness for survival is a thought process all Bunkers experience. This existence, in this broken, destroyed world, is nothing but pain and suffering for all who inhabit it. That is why Nell's people endeavour to save all those they come into contact with. They take on the burden of sacrificing those close to them so that they may find peace in the next life, and in hopes that people across the world will manage to rebuild society and make an astounding comeback from the destruction which plagues the earth. They save people. Yes, they are saved only through death, but Nell can only imagine that it is a sweet relief from the torment brought forth from a poor existence in this world. Nell always says a few words before she plants her dagger into the chest of someone she saves: *Let the next life be kinder than this one.*

It is a small thing, she knows, but she hopes it brings them some peace, and hopes it rings true for them all. She only regrets that she will never experience such kindness for herself. She has saved too many this way to be saved herself. It is a burdensome existence, but it is worth it to buy time for the other people inhabiting this inhospitable planet and to save those she comes into contact with.

Nell straightens to her full height and turns to her people with a bright smile on her face. There is only one way Nell can let Holly live, but it requires her to lie to her people. She is not fond of the idea, but she is curious as to how they will react. Her people and Holly both.

"Friends," she begins. "I bring fantastic news. Holly Mason has made the decision to join us. To follow our scriptures, and to follow our way of life." For a moment, they are all stunned into silence, before everyone begins to whoop and cheer, ecstatic that the damned will be saved, if not by leaving this cruel earth, then at least by helping them save others. That is all they endeavour to do here, after all. Nell and her people are no different than Renee, or Holly, or any of the Bunkers, really, because none of them can face the kind of salvation they bring for others. They cannot be saved themselves, so they help others reach what they will never be able to see with their own eyes.

"What," Holly says, quiet enough that only Nell can hear, but Nell reaches down and places her palm atop Holly's head. Her hair, now less silk-like and more similar to the reeds one might find in a shallow pond, is greasy to the touch. Nell carefully closes her fingers into a fist, like a fly trap plant capturing its prey, and tilts Holly's face up to look at her. Nell looks down, and Holly's confused, searching eyes and open, awed lips bring a smile to Nell's face.

Nell shakes her head. "Do not question it," she says. "I am saving you the only way I can. You will never truly be saved, just like the rest of us, but you can help us save others." She does not wait for Holly to nod her understanding, and instead grips her hair tighter and pushes her face down to the earth. Holly goes, willingly, and presses her nose to the dirt as her people continue cheering and chanting for her, ecstatic at her decision to join their cause. And Nell smiles, because it is a lie only she and Holly know. But neither of them will ever tell the truth, because it would spell certain doom for them both.

CXXII

She hopes Holly at least has the common sense to understand that.

"Let us feast!" Nell says at last, letting Holly up, and turning back to her seat across the clearing. When Constance brings her a cup of berry wine, Nell raises it and looks out to her people where they sit and look up at her with smiles on their faces and identical cups in their hands. "To new friends, to those we have saved, and to those we will save." Her people repeat her words, a chant that washes over Nell and gives her the strength and courage to continue another day. She smiles. And she drinks. And Holly, still kneeling in the mud and dirt in the centre of the clearing, stares up at Nell with nothing but awe and worship in her wide eyes.

TWENTY FIVE

Holly
Day 2
2280 C.E.

W hen the feast ends, Emory walks Holly back to the school and back into the cell where everyone else is waiting. She hears pained groans before she even steps inside the room, and when she does, she spots everyone crowding around Frank. That's right, Holly remembers. The cultists shot him. Everyone turns to look at Holly when she enters the cell, and Irene, uninjured, reaches for her hand.

"Please," Irene begs. "He's in so much pain. Renee, he can't hold on any longer."

Holly swallows against the dryness in her throat and joins everyone on the floor. They part so she can scoot closer to Frank, but as soon as she sees his wound, she recoils, trying not to vomit. Holly places a hand to her lips and looks away. She closes her eyes, but the image of his infected, swollen wound, comes to the forefront of her mind. The sight of it, accompanied by the smell of it, is too overwhelming, and she can't keep her food down. Holly turns further from everybody else and throws up on the cold concrete behind her. She places both hands down to steady herself, and her forearms get splattered in the contents of her stomach. She suddenly feels sickly and sweaty all over. Her back, right down her spine, goes slick, and her hands are clammy when she digs the heel of her palms into her eyes.

"Renee?" Irene asks, placing a cautious hand on her shoulder blade. "Are you alright? What did they do to you?"

She can't bring herself to respond, afraid she'll vomit again if she opens her mouth to answer, so she shakes her head instead.

CXXV

"What's wrong? How can we help?" Asks another voice, and a quick look over her shoulder tells Holly that it's Sonja. She's cradling her broken wrist to her chest and settling Holly with a look of confusion. Maybe suspicion. Holly's not sure. She hopes nobody's caught on to the fact that they're not looking at Renee anymore. She's sure that they will any minute now, though, because they've asked her to perform a medical procedure that Holly doesn't know how to do; but Renee does.

When the scientists who began the Bunker community continued their research and decided to pass on their consciousness to their children upon their eighteenth birthdays, they doomed any and all descendants of theirs to an early death, and stripped them of all possible individuality. They tricked their children and their children's children into believing it was an honour. They didn't know they'd be trapped in their own heads for the rest of their lives. Didn't know it wasn't a true death, because that only happens when your consciousness leaves your body forever. But with the scientists' research, with their transferring of minds into another, the host's consciousness doesn't dissolve, doesn't disappear into nothingness. No. It stays, trapped in the head that was once theirs, now taken over by a parasite. They are resigned to spend the rest of their days shouting from inside a soundproof box, where no one can hear them, not even the parasite that has taken over their body.

So what changed? Why Holly, and why now?

What triggered her to push the boundaries too far, to break out of the prison she'd been confined to these past few years? And where did Renee go? Is she there now, in that cage, destined to watch Holly fuck up everything she'd worked so hard to keep perfect, just the way she wanted?

She's not sure where Renee is now, and she doesn't care. All Holly knows is that she is going to fuck it all up, and she'll barely have to try.

"Renee? What's wrong?" Sonja asks again. Holly swallows the bile, and the remnants of her vomit go with it. The stench of Frank's wound, and now her vomit mixed with it, is still too much. It singes the fine hairs in her nose and the rest of her bile burns the inside of her throat. But she ignores it the best she can as she turns back to where Frank's slumped against the wall and breathing so shallow, so quick, that Holly wonders how he's still alive at all.

"Fra—Pablo," she catches herself, and hopes no one notices her slip up. He doesn't shift his gaze from where it's stuck to his thigh, so she says the scientist's name again. "Pablo. Can you tell me how you feel?" All those years trapped in her own head, watching, listening to Renee treat wounds in the bunker; Holly should have learned how to speak to a patient, at the very least. But she never paid attention. It didn't matter if she did or didn't, she would reason as she sat there in her box, because she'd never get out of there and have to do it herself.

He mutters something under his breath, so quiet Holly can't hear what he's saying. She leans in closer, asks him to repeat what he said. "Kill me, Renee." And it's still too quiet, and she wishes she hadn't heard it. But she did, and she reels back at the sound of it. Frank finally lifts his gaze to meet hers. His eyes are glazed over, he's sweating profusely all along his hairline, and the colour has all but gone out of his face. It would be a mercy kill, Holly understands that. But the thought of killing someone — of killing her *friend* — is so unsettling, a wave of nausea overcomes her, and she squeezes her eyes shut to stave off the feeling. After it's washed away, Holly looks back at Frank, and for a moment, she sees the kid she grew up

CXXVIII

with. He's only two years older than she is. They were friends all throughout their childhood — not to say that she *wasn't* friends with other kids from the bunker, but Frank was always different, always closer, always kinder. It would be a mercy kill, but it would also be killing her best friend. Holly would never be the same again.

She leans forward to Frank and gently cups his face in her hands. He's sweaty, and clammy, but she doesn't care. She looks into his eyes. *Really* looks. Searches for any sign that Frank is really still in there. Of course, she knows he is. But she looks deep into those brown eyes, desperate to find some sign of the man she used to know. At the very least, she hopes he can understand that she's Holly again, not Renee. Hopes Frank understands that when she kills him, she's doing it as a friend, not as a coworker. That in this moment, it is not Renee and Pablo; it is Holly and Frank.

He smiles softly, and Holly doesn't know if Frank has managed what she has, or if Pablo is content to die here. She closes her eyes to get his face out of her mind's eye, and holds out a hand.

"Give me something sharp," she says, so quiet she's not sure if anyone catches it. But then there's a cold weight in her hand, and Holly wraps her fingers around it. She doesn't look as she moves her hand closer to where she knows Frank's chest is, and then, without giving herself the opportunity to back out, to change her mind, she plunges the weapon deep into his heart. The telltale squelching of metal piercing through skin, through muscle, forces Holly's eyes open, and she doesn't realise she's crying until Frank, so weak his eyelids are slipping closed, brings a shaking, heavy hand up to her face and wipes them from her cheeks.

I'm sorry, Holly thinks, and she pushes the blade deeper. Frank lets out a short, phlegmy gasp, and then his eyes go glassy and unresponsive. His hand drops to his side. His head rolls away and he stares off somewhere over Holly's left shoulder. But he's not staring. He's dead. She closes her eyes again, lets go of the blade, and cries.

"Renee?" This from Nikolai, who's sitting in front of her. Their furrowed brow and slightly parted lips tell her they know. They understand what's happened, even if they can't understand how. Their eyes go wide, and Holly closes hers again as they say, more than ask; breathe, more than say, "Holly."

"What?" Sonja asks, incredulity thick in her voice. "No, that's not possible."

CXXX

Holly listens as the group — what's left of them — argue about the possibility that they are speaking to the person who's body their beloved medic took over more than a year ago. She doesn't open her eyes, doesn't look at them as they discuss her like she's nothing more than a statistic, an anomaly in the way of perfecting their research.

Someone grabs her chin and turns her face towards them. She finally opens her eyes and comes face to face with Lee. His grip is firm, if not a little bruising. He's scowling at her, his eyes roaming all over her face, searching for something, a singular answer to his likely millions of questions.

"What is my name?" He asks at last. Holly swallows her nerves. She's not sure what he wants her to say; would saying his real name shock him enough to believe it? Or would it make him lash out? Lee's in his early thirties, so she's known him as both himself and the parasitic scientist in his mind for long enough that she could call him Lee or Joey and she'd believe it herself.

But she decides to go with the answer she thinks he wants to hear, and says, "Lee." Just like Nikolai before him, Lee's eyes go wide, and he drops her chin in favour of moving away from her face.

CXXXI

"Holy shit," says Sandra. "You really aren't Renee. How the fuck did that happen?" And really, Holly's not sure herself. She doesn't say so, and doesn't shrug. She just looks around at them all staring at her, takes them all in. These aren't the people she knows, the people she grew up with. They haven't been for a long time.

"I think the real question we should be asking is *when* the fuck did that happen?" Nikolai asks. They shrug. "I mean, we're not going to be able to figure out how it happened while we're in here, but if we figure out the when, maybe that could lead us to the how."

"Right," Sonja nods. "So, Holly — god, it feels so weird saying that — when did you, how do I word this? Take over? Come back out?"

"When did you kill Renee?" Sandra mutters to herself, but the room is otherwise quiet, so Holly catches it.

"*You* tried to kill *me*," Holly says, hoping the hatred she feels for these people right now comes through in her words. "You tricked me into believing it was an honour to take one of you into my head. You think *we* are the ones who die. But we don't die. We're stuck in our own minds. We can see and hear everything you see when you're in our heads, but we can't do anything about it."

CXXXII

"You're avoiding the question," says Irene. Holly levels her with a glare. She never liked Irene. They're the same age, had been infested for almost the same length of time. The Bunker likes competition between their children, and Holly and Irene were always put against each other when they were younger.

"Fuck you," Holly spits. Irene's eyes go wide, because it's *not* Irene, and Renee and Aoife get along just fine. The only upper hand she ever had against Irene is that her birthday is two weeks before Irene's, so she became infested first. She'd thought it an honour, at first, but it hadn't taken long to realise it was worse than all her worst nightmares.

"Answer the question," Lee prompts, and sighs. He pinches the bridge of his nose, as if her refusal to answer is the reason he's so tired.

Holly sighs. "Only a few hours ago. And I don't think your precious medic is dead. She's probably stuck in my head now, just like I was. Karma, I guess." She tilts her head to one side and the beginnings of a smile grace her lips. "But would you like to know who's definitely alive? My mother."

"Sorry?" Nikolai sputters, their eyes wide. "The Renee before you? She's alive?"

"She's here," Holly nods. "And her name is Addison. And mine is *not* Renee."

Lee waves his hand, like he's swatting her words out of the air, dismissing them as unimportant. "Semantics," he says. "She's alive, and she's here. Why? How?"

She only brought it up to get a rise out of them, but their genuine interest is intriguing. Obviously they care about her mother enough to ask about her, but *why*? They hadn't cared about her when they'd implanted all — or, apparently, not all — of her memories as Renee into Holly's brain a little over a year ago. They hadn't cared about her when they told a fourteen year-old Holly that her mother had been caught by the cultists, that there was no way she would survive her trip there.

"Why do you care?" Holly asks.

"You clearly thought we would if you cared enough to bring it up." Nikolai shrugs with their one good shoulder.

"No, I didn't think you would." Holly shakes her head. "I thought you'd deny it, say I was lying. I thought you'd care more about the fact that I'*m* here."

"While your unexpected presence is intriguing," Sandra admits. "I think the fact that one of us has survived, what, five years here is at least equally interesting." The others nod their agreement.

"And besides," Irene adds. "She's still Renee. We could use one of them right about now." Holly scowls at her again, more for insulting her inability to stitch them up if they get hurt again than the agreement that Holly isn't an interesting case to them. They're scientists, after all. This was their field of interest before the end of the world. Why are they more fascinated by her mother being alive than they are by the fact that Holly has returned after more than a year of them thinking she'd died off in her own head?

Does Holly's mother have access to information they want? Does she know something they don't? Have they somehow caught on to the fact that she erased some of her memories as Renee? Do they want to punish her for it? Holly can't think of anything else that would warrant this level of interest.

"Can you bring Renee back?" Sonja asks in the brief, uncomfortable quiet that settles over them like a layer of dust over undisturbed furniture. Everyone turns to look at her. She blinks at the attention and clears her throat before repeating her question.

"Why would I do that?" Holly asks. "Even if I could, which I'm not sure is possible, I don't know what would happen to me. I don't even know how I came back."

"She was trying to get us out of here," Irene says. "I don't understand how she thought she was going to do that by killing Harriet, or by telling us all to get all friendly with the cultists while she screamed at them herself. But she said she was trying to get us out, and I believed her."

"You know you're not getting out of here alive, right? You know they're going to kill you." Holly frowns, because are they *really* this dense? This naïve? Surely not. They've survived two hundred years in this world. Surely they understand there are some things you just don't walk away from.

"What about you?" Lee asks. "You didn't say, 'we're not getting out of here alive.' You said, 'you're not getting out of here alive.' What about you?"

She doesn't know if she should tell them that Nell's accepted her into this community. She doesn't know if she should tell them that it was a decision made with no input on her behalf, or that she doesn't want to join them at all, even if it means survival. Because a life with these cultists isn't a life worth living. They're murderers, they're savages. She closes her eyes and sees Elias, strung up

CXXXVI

between two trees. She sees them cutting him down, flaying him like an animal and starting a fire in front of where she knelt in the clearing to roast chunks of his flesh. She'd rather kill herself, deprive them of the satisfaction of sacrificing her for their cause, than live with them for any longer than she has to.

But then again, maybe she can win over their trust, make them believe she really is following their scriptures, and help the Bunkers escape. Would she die as a consequence? Would it be worth it? She's not one of these scientists; she can't weigh up the variables, the possible positive and negative outcomes that would occur as a result of trying something like this. But she does know one thing: If she fucks it up, she's dead.

TWENTY SIX

Nell
12 Weeks
199 P.A.

T he day after the feast, Nell stands outside the cell where Holly and the rest of her friends sit or slump or sleep on the floor and against the concrete walls. She clasps her hands together and clears her throat, and all but one of them opens their eyes. Nell narrows hers at the man slumped against the wall, his shirt stained crimson, and purses her lips as she flicks her gaze to Holly where she sits up at the man's right side. She wonders, briefly, if this is not Holly at all, if Renee is trying to play a trick on her, to convince her that she is who Nell wants her to be. But then Holly's eyes lock onto Nell's, and she knows that it is not true. That this really *is* Holly. She has been crying. Tear tracks line her cheeks, and her eyes are red and puffy. Renee did not cry when she senselessly murdered one of her companions; Holly is crying in the aftermath of killing a friend.

"Holly," Nell calls. "Come with me." Holly looks around at the others in the cell with her. They all nod. She gets to her feet and crosses the room, a slight limp in her step and a small wince in her face that she mostly manages to conceal.

They walk the halls in silence, and only when they make it outside does Nell speak. "Why is your friend dead?" She asks. Holly looks sideways at her, and Nell raises an eyebrow.

"He was going to die of an infection anyway," Holly says quietly. She brings her shoulders up to her ears and looks down at the ground while she walks. Nell cannot tell if it is an attempt to focus, so she does not trip over the little rocks in the earth, or if it is sadness over the loss of a friend.

CXXXIX

"Did you kill him?" Nell asks, and stops walking. Holly does too, and Nell waits for her to speak. It is windy today, and Holly's long hair whips around her face. Only days ago had Nell been envious of the silk-like texture of that hair. Now it is no different to her own, and she feels a little vindicated. This is proof that Holly really is just like Nell and everybody else here. She cannot hide behind the façade of Renee Clarke anymore. But something tells Nell that it was never a choice she could make for herself in the first place.

"I had to," Holly whispers, and looks back at the ground. "They thought I was Renee. They thought I could save him." She sniffs. "But I couldn't."

"Was he a good friend of yours, or simply an acquaintance, Holly?" Nell asks. Holly sniffs again and looks back up at her. There are fresh tears in her eyes that threaten to spill over onto her cheeks. Nell reaches over to wipe them away, but Holly flinches back and turns her face away. Then she turns back to Nell, her eyes saucer-wide and panic stricken, as if she expects Nell to hit her for moving away.

"Who was he to you, Holly? Tell me." Nell says.

It takes Holly a few moments to get the words out the way she wants them to sound, and then she says, "He was my best friend. And I killed him." She swipes away the tears forming in her eyes and sniffs one last time as she looks back up at Nell. "There's nothing I can do about it now, though. He's gone. I have to accept that and move on."

"He is not truly gone, Holly Mason," Nell shakes her head. Holly frowns.

"How do you know—"

"I have grown quite close with your mother these past five years," Nell smiles. Holly nods, though by the look in her eyes, she is not really here. Her mind is elsewhere. Perhaps with her friend she has killed. Perhaps she is thinking of her mother. But Nell cannot read minds, she can only tell them what to do.

"What did you mean, he's not really gone?" Holly asks, furrowing her brows. "Because I know everyone always says when people die they're still with us in our hearts, or whatever. But I have a feeling you mean it differently than that."

Nell nods. "Come, this way. I will explain." She gestures for Holly to follow, and Nell leads her to the log seats where she has sat with Renee for the last three days. It is odd, seeing the exact same face, the exact same body, while knowing there is a different mind inside it. How did

Holly kill Renee's consciousness in her head? How did Holly not die, trapped in her own head? Nell does not ask these questions. Instead, she answers Holly's.

"Your friend, though he unfortunately passed before we could save him, will still have a chance at redemption in the afterlife." Nell explains. "Here, with our scriptures, we believe that sacrificing a person you are close with, no matter whether you follow the scriptures or not, gives them a chance to experience the true happiness after their death."

"How does he do that, then?" Holly asks, readjusting her position on the log seat, hoping to be more comfortable.

"He does not have to do anything," Nell says. She brushes a stray hair out of her face where the wind had blown it out of the braid at the back of her head. "He cannot do anything. Not anymore. He is dead, after all."

"Right," says Holly, under her breath.

"It is up to you to make this right now, Holly."

Holly looks up. "Me?"

"You killed him, did you not?"

She looks away again, but mutters a quiet, "Yes."

"Then it is your responsibility to make this right. It is up to you to save his soul before it is too late."

CXLII

Holly's eyes are wild and desperate, searching for answers. "How do I do that?" She all but demands. Nell tilts her head and smiles again.

"You must follow our scriptures. You must turn your life here into something that will convince whatever waits for us after we die that what you did was in service of our cause. Only then may his soul be saved." Holly purses her lips in consideration.

"What about me?" She asks. The words come out quiet and shaky, like she is afraid of the answer. The wind blows the words away on a soft breeze.

Nell hums. She asks, "Can I ask you a question about Renee Clarke?" Holly swallows and nods. "When she had taken over your mind, could you still see what she saw? Hear what she heard?"

Holly nods again. "Then you already know the answer to your question." Nell leans forward, so close to Holly's face that there is no misunderstanding when she says, "You will never see your friend again. You will never reach the true happiness after death that we bring others by saving them. But you will not be alone." Nell reaches for Holly's chin. She grasps it gently in her hand and tilts Holly's chin up to look Nell in the eye.

Nell smiles. "I will be with you every step of the way."

TWENTY SEVEN

Renee
2 Days
2280 C.E.

O h, God. Is this what it was like for you, Holly? This whole time? I don't think I can last as long as you did.

Please, Holly. I'm sorry. I want to stop this. I want to make sure they can't put me inside anyone's head ever again.

Please, Holly.

Please.

TWENTY EIGHT

Holly
Day 2
2280 C.E.

N ell leads her through the hallways of the building and past the room Holly's friends are being kept. She takes her past the half-rotted sign that says 'Re...pt...n' and through where they've torn down a pair of wide double-doors that lead out into a small, circular atrium, where, on a sunny day, light would stream in through the glass dome ceiling. There are broken and shattered sections of the ceiling, but it is mostly intact. Ten to fifteen of Nell's cultists mill about the room, tending to tasks and speaking in hushed conversations. It is a bit breezy in here, with the missing sections of ceiling, but it is significantly warmer than it is outside.

When the cultists spot Nell, they stop their busy-body activities and turn to her with a slight nod, which she returns, a small smile on her lips. "Friends," she calls out, and the sound echoes in the wide, tall space. "Please, join me in welcoming Holly Mason to our community."

Everyone in the atrium, in a chorus of voices of all registers across all octaves, speaks, "Welcome, Holly Mason." It sounds like a drone, and Holly can never quite be sure where each sound is coming from. The fine hairs on the back of her neck stands on end as the sound makes its way to her ears and echoes in her skull as if it is empty. She doesn't flinch, though, and tries not to let her discomfort show on her face, for fear of Nell sniffing it out like a tracker dog.

Nell turns that smile on Holly, and it is anything but comforting. But Holly can't have Nell thinking that is how she sees it, so she smiles back and hopes it is not as shaky as she feels. Nell places a hand on Holly's shoulder that she probably thinks is comforting, but Holly's skin crawls at the point of contact, and she wants to tear her arm away from Nell's hand. But she can't. she has to keep up this façade as long as she can. As long as Nell believes it.

"Come, this way." Nell says, and without a second thought, Holly does. They walk through the atrium, and through the doorway with no doors with a sign above it that reads 'Au...i...rium.' They walk down another dimly lit hallway, only supplied with light by the atrium at their backs and the few lit candles on the floor of the corridor. Mostly-corroded metal cubby holes line the walls here, but Nell keeps walking onward, so Holly continues too.

At last they reach double doors which haven't been removed from their frames, and Nell pulls them open and ushers Holly through. This room is larger than the atrium, but its walls do not reach quite as high. There is no glass in the ceiling, and in fact, there is very little glass in here at all. The room is mostly shrouded in darkness, and when Nell lets the doors close behind her, the lack of light becomes almost suffocating, like it is trying to crawl into Holly's mouth. Down her throat, infecting her lungs. Taking up all the space and leaving no room for air. She takes a deep breath, tries to combat this feeling, but all it does is invite more darkness into her body. This time it attacks her blood vessels, snaking its way through her capillaries, her arteries and veins, until it reaches her heart to stop it beating.

"Holly?" Nell asks, and her voice is muffled to Holly's ears. She gasps for air she can't take in, and she falls to her knees. The floor is made of wood, and her knees smack against it, *hard.*

A hand rests on Holly's shoulder, and she flinches away involuntarily from the touch. Holly squeezes her eyes shut, desperate for a different, familiar kind of darkness, but this one just mimics that which is outside her. There is a buzzing in her ears, like hundreds — no, *thousands* — of flies, or bees, or hell, even wasps flying straight into her eardrums, bursting through and continuing to her brain. Maybe they'll get in there and eat up all the grey matter, all the tissue that lets her think, and feel, and live. Holly sends out a futile wish for them to kill Renee while they're at it.

Then there is light, and Holly peels her eyelids open. Across the hall, to her left: A door has been thrown open to let in sunlight from outside, and she gasps air into her lungs as she begins crawling on her hands and knees towards it. Like a moth to a flame, or a soul to the afterlife. She is still heaving for gasps of air when she makes it to the other side of the hall, and only when she is outside, on her back, staring up at the grey clouds above, does Holly finally closes her eyes and feels the muscles in her shoulders relax.

"Holly?" Nell asks as she comes to stand over her. Holly prises open her eyelids once more and looks up at Nell where she is blocking her view of the clouds above. There is something akin to worry on Nell's face. Maybe more like concern, or confusion. Holly can't tell. Her vision is a little blurry. But she sits up and gets to shaky feet before Nell can question her any further.

Holly dusts off her pants and clears her throat. She tucks a strand of hair behind her ear and looks at the dusty earth beneath her feet. "I'm sorry," she says. "I didn't mean to—"

"It is alright, Holly," Nell shakes her head, pulling Holly's gaze back up to Nell's face. Nell is smiling. "There is no need to apologise. I should be the one apologising. I was not aware you would have such a reaction to the darkness of the hall."

Neither was Holly, but she doesn't voice that. She doesn't know why she reacted like that. It is embarrassing, more than anything else. She is supposed to be getting close to these people, gaining their trust, finding a way to escape before all her friends are sacrificed, but how is she supposed to do that when she is keeling over every time she is in the dark? She is not a child anymore. She shouldn't be so afraid of the dark. She never was, which is the oddest part of it all. Why now? Why here? Holly wonders, idly, if Renee was afraid of the dark. Wonders if that fear lingers in her body still, even after Holly regained control over the gearstick that controls it.

"Was that room what you wanted to show me?" Holly asks, and Nell doesn't answer at first. Then she hums and nods.

"In part." Nell says, "I wanted to introduce you to where people are saved, but it can wait until tomorrow, when it is lit up." She smiles. "I read somewhere that the expression is 'Like a Christmas tree,' but I do not know what that is, so I think I will leave it at that."

Holly nods once, and Nell turns her attention away from her. She glances off somewhere behind Holly's shoulder, and some kind of realisation crosses her features before she turns back to Holly with a wider smile.

"Would you like to see your mother?" Nell asks, and Holly's jaw drops a little.

Of course, she was there, in her own mind, when Renee met Holly's mother, Renee's predecessor. But she couldn't interact with her, couldn't say anything or do anything. She wants, more than anything else right now, to see her mother. To give her a hug so tight it squeezes her ribs to creaking and never let go. So she nods, and if it is possible, Nell's smile grows again. It is not ingenuine, and it never has been, which is the most unsettling part of it all. She always means the emotions behind that smile, whenever she shows it to anyone.

"Alright then," Nell nods. "That is what we shall do. Follow me."

TWENTY NINE

Holly
Day 2
2280 C.E.

S he doesn't look like her mother. Not really. In all the ways that matter, maybe, but there is something wrong, something fundamentally *off* about the woman sitting in front of Holly that she can't quite place. It is unnerving, and she wants to figure out what it is, but she can't put her finger to just what is so *wrong* about her.

When she turns from the table to face Holly, a glimmer crosses her eyes that Holly doesn't think is hope. No. It is fear, as plain and obvious as the sun in the sky. Fear that she is looking at Renee again, that the violence Renee enacted upon Nell when she was here yesterday will occur again. It is there in her face, and it is unavoidable, and it hurts Holly's heart to look at. She winces and fights the urge to look away.

Nell speaks for her. "Addison," she says. "This is Holly, not Renee." Holly's mother frowns and puts down the cracked plant pot she's holding. She peels off her gloves and sets those aside, too, and then takes a tentative step towards Holly and Nell. Her eyes don't even consider Nell as she approaches. They're fixed on Holly, on searching every feature of her face, as if there is a physical difference between Holly and Renee. They both know there is not, just like Holly knows the woman who gently places her calloused hands on her face is at once her mother and not her mother. But Holly only ever knew her mother as Renee, never the name Nell refers to her as now, and as she looks upon her, she is torn between the two. *Addison. Renee.* Neither quite seem to fit the features she is staring at, too similar to her own to deny the familial connection between them, but so different from the expression of love and care Holly once knew that it is like looking into the face of a complete stranger.

Has her mother managed what she has, then? Is this really Addison? Really the person she was before she became Renee Clarke? Or is Nell simply refusing to call her Renee, like she had the second she found out that the name Holly was hiding behind Renee?

"My baby," her mother says, her voice no louder than a whisper and breaking at the edges. And Holly knows, with those two words, that this really is not the woman she used to know. Her mother would never call her that. Would never say those words and sound so weak when she says them. But she stays still and lets Addison search her face for something like love, and when she doesn't find it, the slight smile on the face of the woman who was once her mother disappears, and she steps back.

"Holly," Addison whispers as tears fill her eyes to the brim. "Holly, it's me. It's your mother."

Holly swallows the guilt and the shame and the tears building behind her own walls as she shakes her head. "No, you're not her. You're who she was." She shakes her head again and steps away from her mother. "I don't know you."

CLIV

And that seems to be the final straw for Addison, because the tears begin to fall from her eyes and she clamps a hand over her mouth to catch the sob that erupts from her mouth as she falls to the ground. Holly watches, and sniffs back tears of her own as her not-mother breaks down in front of her. It is strange, she thinks as she looks down at Addison. This woman recognises her as her own child, but Holly cannot see Addison as her mother. She doesn't think she'll ever be able to. It doesn't matter how much she looks identical to the woman Holly knows is her mother, doesn't matter that it is the same body, that Addison was stuck in her own head for so many more years than Holly was stuck in hers. Addison Mason is not Holly's mother. But Renee Clarke is.

Holly has only ever known her mother by that name. Has only ever referred to her as such, has only ever known that personality in this body she looks down upon, crumbled on the floor of the greenhouse. Holly doesn't know Addison, doesn't know this mind, can't bring herself to want to learn. It won't matter in a few days anyway, if she can manage the impossible. And if she fails it won't matter, either, because she'll be dead. Either way, as Holly

CLV

watches this woman break down in front of her, she can't help but feel a little empty inside.

Someone places their hand on her shoulder and a quick look to the side alerts Holly to Nell's presence. She is looking at her with curiosity in her eyes, and something like understanding, or pride, too. Holly takes a deep breath in and wipes away any and all remnants of tears that might have slipped out without her knowing.

"Can we go?" She whispers to Nell, but in the greenhouse, where the only other sound is Addison's sobs continue to wrack her body as she shakes with the tears, the sound travels as quickly and as loud as a clap of thunder. Nell nods once, slowly, and with a gentle hand at the small of Holly's back, leads her out of the greenhouse. Addison's sobs ring in the back of Holly's mind as she walks away, but she pushes the sound from her mind. Addison made her choice. She is not Holly's concern any longer.

CLVI

THIRTY

Renee
2 Days
2280 C.E.

No. Renee. Get up. Oh, fuck. This isn't happening. This can't be happening.

Holly, she'll kill you. Please, let me help you. Let me out.

How did you get out of here in the first place? How did you manage it?

It doesn't make sense. There's no failsafe in the science.

How did you get out, Holly?

Please, I need to know. You can't get out of there yourself.

You need my help, Holly.

Please.

THIRTY ONE

Nell
12 Weeks
199 P.A.

Nell tries to conceal the joy she is feeling as she leads Holly away from her mother. It is a difficult task, of course, but knowing that Holly feels no connection to her life with the Bunkers will make her acclimation all the more effortless. She will slot into the ranks so incredibly seamlessly; Nell is sure of it. She does not have the gifts, as Nell does, as Marlowe did. But perhaps, if she holds enough conviction, enough belief in their cause and their scriptures, Holly may one day be able to stand at Nell's side and have rightfully earned her place.

The relief that washes over Nell is palpable, and it has her standing more upright than usual. Never before has she met a Renee Clarke that became who she was before. Never before has she met a Bunker that was even remotely interested in her scriptures. But maybe that is because she has never before met a true Bunker, only ever the parasites that lived before the catastrophe that sent the world into desolation, hundreds of years before Nell's birth. Nell has met four Renee Clarkes in her time; never before have they surprised her as this one has.

Even before the return of Holly's mind to her body, Nell had been intrigued. She always was, by Renee Clarke. There was something about her, right from the very first one she met, that was different than her companions. It was not that she has always been so opposed to Nell's beliefs, but rather that she has always voiced them so strongly. With the exception of Addison, Renee Clarke has been an angry individual, full of a rage Nell has never been able to understand. She has tried, of course, tried her best to poke and prod at Renee like if she digs just so, just deep enough, she will learn something interesting, will understand why Renee, of all the Bunkers, is so outspoken about her hatred of Nell and her people. But she has never found the root of the plant of hatred within Renee Clarke.

She leads Holly back to the atrium, and past it through the archway with '...*br...y*' written above it. Down the hall and through the doors to the right, and then they are in the library, full of stacks upon stacks and shelves upon shelves of books. Nell thinks she must have read all of them, but she knows that is not possible. There are too many books in this room, it is so expansive, that she cannot possibly have read them all. And she is overwhelmed, every time she finds herself in the library, with the helpless feeling that she will never read enough of those books, that the proportion that she has read will never come close to the total amount of books in this room alone. Most of the time, she tries not to think about how many books there are, out in the world, that survived the bombs that destroyed the earth. Even more, she tries not to think about how many books were burnt and destroyed by the bombs, because the thought of a loss of so much invaluable information has the tendency to sadden her to the point of immobility.

"What are we doing in here?" Holly asks, her voice quiet and a little shaky. She looks around the huge space with awe in her eyes, as if she has never seen a room so big before. Nell does not doubt it; surely no room in the bunker Holly has lived in for her entire life can be so large as this library.

"I like to come here when I become too overwhelmed by things outside." Nell explains. "When I need some time alone to think, without anyone else interrupting me." Holly nods.

Nell read, once, that libraries are supposed to be quiet spaces, where people can come to sit and read in peace. This library is not so quiet, but she attributes it mostly to the gaping hole in the middle of the far wall that lets in the wind and rain. None of the books are ever kept too close to that wall, for fear of the weather damaging the brittle pages. Instead, they are stored in heavy shelves and tall stacks near the library's entrance, in four long, neat rows. One can enter the library, scan the shelves for something to read, and make their way further into the large room to sit and read. The system works, and it has been in place for almost as long as their community here has existed. Nell is proud of the upkeep she has helped enforce within the community, and especially so within the library.

"Would you like to read something, or would simply sitting together suffice?" Nell asks Holly when she does not say anything else. Holly tears her gaze away from the shelves upon shelves overfilling with reading material and her eyes land back on Nell's face with an admiring glint.

"I think I'd like to sit and talk, if that's alright," says Holly. Nell nods and leads her further into the space, where they find two chairs. Nell settles in, and it takes Holly a little longer to get comfortable.

When they have settled, Nell asks, "Why do you not see Addison as your mother?" Holly gives her an indecipherable look, which surprises Nell, as she can often read people's expressions rather well. Then Holly looks down to her hands where she has begun fiddling with the once more blood-stained fabric of her shirt. She licks her lips as she thinks of what to say, and Nell is content to sit in the silence and watch as Holly forms her thoughts.

"I don't know if this will make sense to you," Holly begins, speaking slowly. "But I don't see Addison as my mother because she's not. That body gave birth to me, yes. But not that person. Renee is my mother; Addison is not." She looks up at Nell, her eyebrows furrowing slightly in consideration. "Does that make sense?"

It does not, but Nell nods anyway. Tension bleeds out of Holly's shoulders and she lets out a sigh. She presses her thumb and forefinger to the bridge of her nose and says, "I can't look at her and see my mother, even though I know, technically, she is."

"Would you prefer it if you did not see her at all from now on?" Nell asks, and Holly turns that inquisitive look on her.

"What?" She asks.

Nell readjusts in her seat. "I can arrange for Addison to stay out of any places you will ever find yourself. This community thrives off of cooperation — I believe it is essential for human survival in this decimated world, for if we are not able to cooperate with the people we live with, what chance is there of making it through the trials and tribulations we face every day? We cannot do it alone, so we must work together. If Addison will be a problem for your cooperation in this community moving forward, I can look into arranging your schedules around this." Like magnets, Nell thinks idly. Holly and Addison are too alike, the same charge of a magnet, and should never interact for fear of unstable results to their cooperation within the community at large.

In fact, perhaps there should be no possible opportunity for them to interact, ever again. The community has had Addison's Renee Clarke for five years now. Maybe it is time for a new Renee Clarke to help them move through this world, one who is more receptive and accepting of their ways. Addison has never made it a secret that she does not wholly approve of their methods of survival, of their saving others through sacrifice. But Nell may yet be able to win Holly over to their cause, if she manages to do so before her friends' saving ceremony tomorrow evening. The event is rapidly approaching, and Nell has very little time, but she thinks that if she can convince Holly that they will be better off in whatever world awaits them on the other side of this, perhaps it will be time for Addison Mason to leave them, too. She will never find the salvation that the rest of the Bunkers will, just like any other Renee Clarke. But perhaps she deserves something different than this life, even if it is no better than the one she has now.

"Maybe," Holly mutters. She looks down at her hands once more.

"Holly," Nell says. "May I ask what Bunkers believe happens to a person when they die?"

Holly frowns again and shrugs before answering. "That we're just gone. There's nothing after you die. Just death, and then nothing." She looks up at Nell with raised eyebrows. "I suspect you're about to tell me what *you* believe happens."

Nell nods. "We believe that someone who has been saved, who we have helped find salvation, will find something better after death. We do not know exactly what that entails, of course, because once you die, there is no coming back, and because none of us here will ever experience such a freedom from pain."

"So what do you think happens to you, specifically?" Holly asks.

"We do not know." Nell shrugs one shoulder. "Really, it is not so different a belief to the one you have grown up with. It is only that we try to save others that differs from your friends' belief."

"That's interesting," Holly says quietly. "Will you tell me more?"

"Like what?" Nell says, a small smile spreading across her face. She is already winning Holly over, and she has barely done anything to try.

CLXVI

"Anything about your beliefs." Holly looks into Nell's eyes, and pure, unadulterated curiosity gazes up at Nell. It is almost too easy, but Nell will take that curiosity and turn it into pure belief like Holly's mind is the wool at the spinning wheel that Nell uses to spin fine thread.

"Alright," Nell nods. And so she tells Holly all she has told Renee these past few days, in case there was anything Holly missed, anything she did not absorb into her own thoughts and consciousness. She tells Holly all that and more; about the community's beliefs surrounding death, and life, and what comes next. About the saving ceremony, when Holly asks what her friends will experience, and everything that it entails. The only thing Nell does not tell her is that her friends' saving ceremony is scheduled for tomorrow evening, that it can only be put off for so long, especially with only twelve weeks left until the second catastrophe is set to arrive. If they are to postpone such an event, they will need to save Holly's friends as soon as possible. There are only twelve weeks to prepare, twelve weeks to postpone the inevitable, twelve weeks to death. At the end of this week, there will only be eleven left, but for now there are twelve.

And Nell will not risk everything they have built here over so many generations to help Holly get more acquainted to the community. The saving ceremony must happen tomorrow, and it must work. Nell will not die in twelve weeks. Her community will not die in twelve weeks. And neither will Holly, because she is part of the community now; Nell can see the acceptance in her eyes as she nods along and asks more questions. The wool of Holly's mind has become the obedient thread, ready to be used at the sole discretion of the weaver, and Nell is prepared to use that thread for everything she could ever need of it.

THIRTY TWO

Holly
Day 2
2280 C.E.

W hen Nell returns Holly to the cell, there is a bone-deep terror within her that only amplifies when she is locked in with the rest of her companions. Frank has been removed, but the blood stains remain where Holly plunged that blade into his heart, the only evidence that he ever existed at all. She thinks about Nell's explanation of her beliefs around death, and wonders if there is any truth to it. If Frank really will find something better in death, or whatever comes after, if anything at all. She cannot bring herself to think he will suffer. It is much too heartbreaking to think about her oldest and dearest friend suffering any more than he did in his last few days. So she hopes Nell is right, even though it terrifies her to feed into the beliefs of this place, because at least it means Frank will find peace.

As soon as she is back, sitting on the concrete floor as far from the stains of Frank's blood as she can possibly get, Irene and Lee corner her. They ask too many questions about what Nell wanted, about what they spoke of, about whether or not Holly has found a way to escape yet. She listens, her whole body numb, and stares blankly at the place where Frank lay only hours ago. He was still here when she left, so someone must have collected his body while she was with Nell. Part of her wants to get up, to go to the bars of her cell and beg the guards to let her see what they have done with Frank. But she knows they would not let her see him, so she stays where she is and finally drags her gaze back to Irene and Lee, who are staring at her expectantly, waiting for her to give them answers to their incessant questions.

CLXX

The first thing she says is, "She's not Renee anymore." Irene and Lee frown and look at each other, wondering what she is talking about, and level her with questioning expressions. "She's done what I have. She's not Renee anymore. She's Addison again."

"Your mother?" Irene asks, and the flinch Holly cannot hold back is enough of an answer. Irene curses under her breath and brings her thumb up to her lips to bite the nail there.

"She's on their side?" Lee asks. Holly is not sure, really, if Addison would say that she is on the cultists' side of this, but she nods anyway, because she does know that Addison cannot be saved. She will not come back with them when they escape this place. *If* they escape, Holly reminds herself.

"How long do we have?" Lee asks. "They're going to kill us, we know that. So we have to get out of here before they do."

"Why would she tell me that? Why would she make us panic? It would only be more of a hassle for them if we tried to escape so blatantly." Holly sighs. "I don't know how long we have, but it can't be long."

"We need to get out tonight." Irene says, her words harsh and quiet. "We can do it. You know how to get outside, yes? They never took us outside, only to the atrium. You can get us out, though. You know how."

She does know her way through the halls, that is true. She could, theoretically, get them out of here. But how do they get back to the bunker from there? How do they make their way through the forest without their torchlights and their navigational devices? They cannot do it, Holly is sure. They would make it ten steps into the forest and already be lost.

"Not tonight," Holly shakes her head. "Let me try and find some of our equipment tomorrow, if they haven't destroyed it already, and then we'll go. We need to know where we're going when we get out of here, and we won't know if we just barge out of here blindly now."

"But we *can* get out of here," Irene says. She tucks a straggly piece of hair behind her ear. None of them have washed themselves in days, and it is beginning to show in their appearance. The smell hit days ago, but now the most prominent scent in this cell is that of Frank's blood and Holly's vomit, also uncleaned from the concrete floor.

"We can all walk," Irene clarifies. She sends a quick look behind her to Sandra, who's asleep across the cell, joined by Sonja and Nikolai, also slumped against the wall behind them. Irene sighs and turns back with an almost imperceptible shake of the head. "I can help her walk out of here. She says it doesn't hurt much anymore, so it won't be too much work for me."

"Just because we can physically walk out of here doesn't mean we can actually make it out." Lee says, and Holly nods, because it is true. "Ren—Holly's right. We should wait until we have some of our gear back. A navigational device, at the very least. We'd be going in completely blind to an area they know like the back of their hands if we just stepped out right now without knowing where we're actually going."

Irene's sigh is all frustration, and it sparks some long-festering grudge in Holly, but she keeps her mouth shut as she reminds herself — as she has had to do since she found herself back in control of her body — that this is *not* Irene. That it is Aoife, and just because it still looks like Irene does not mean that it is.

Emory brings them food and instructs them all to, "Still," as she unlocks the cell's door and slides the tray of enough food for only one person across the concrete. When the cell is locked again, they are freed from the spell keeping them from jumping up and attacking Emory, and Irene jumps for the tray. She divides it into six relatively equal portions, and heads for Sandra, Nikolai, and Sonja first, rousing them from their sleep to offer them food. By the time she makes it back to Holly and Lee, the amount of food on the tray has halved, and she offers it up like a knight might have done with a sword to a king about to be knighted in one of those storybooks Holly's mother used to read to her as a child.

They eat in silence, and then, after a while, Lee says, "I think it'll be soon." Holly and Irene look up at him, and he sighs. "I think they'll kill us soon. A few days, at most." And Holly understands how his mind went there after the food, because the portion sizes they are being fed are not nearly large enough to sustain them for any longer than a week. Holly can already see the signs of malnourishment in her companions. Chief of all that they are beginning to lack the definition in their muscles that they once had. Which means they need to escape sooner than they really should, because if they get any weaker they will not be able to defend themselves against any attack. Their stamina is probably already ruined from days of sitting in confinement and being fed so little, so they will also likely require weapons of some kind. But the only things Holly knows for a fact the cultists here have as weapons are bow and arrows and knives. None of them in here know how to shoot an arrow, and a knife would be so ineffectual against a bow that it is almost laughable.

She understands that it will be near impossible for them to escape, and yet she is trying anyway. Why? Why is it so ingrained in the human psyche to survive? To endure hardship with the hope that they will come out on the other side, still alive if not unharmed? They are social creatures, yes, but really it can only go so far before they should know that their efforts are fruitless.

"Tomorrow, then," Holly says with a nod. "I'll find our things and we can escape tomorrow night."

THIRTY THREE

Renee
2 Days
2280 C.E.

Y ou won't make it. Holly, you won't make it.

Please, I can get us out of there. I can get everyone home.

I promise I'll stop them from putting me in anyone else's heads.

Holly, please. It's the only way. You have to see that.

Please.

THIRTY FOUR

Nell
12 Weeks
199 P.A.

H olly smiles when Nell approaches the cell, and Nell cannot help but smile back. It is nice to see that expression on Holly's face. On a face so similar to the Renee Clarkes that came before her. The ones Nell never got through to the way she has with Holly.

"Holly," Nell says, extending her arm through the open doorway. The rest of her companions have not been told to stay where they are, but they remain seated on the concrete anyway. The two seated with Holly stare at Nell, and the three on the other side of the cell glance warily at Holly. Nell pays them no mind. They are not important to her, not right now. "Come with me." Holly gets to her feet, a struggle even these days later, and walks over to Nell with only the slightest limp in her gait.

Nell leads her toward the atrium. It is raining today, and the holes in the glass roof let the fat drops of water splatter all over the cracked tile, making it slippery to walk on. But they skirt around the edges of the room, as everyone else does, and continue on to the dark hall at the end of the corridor. When they reach it, Nell stops with her hand on the door, and turns to Holly.

"Do you think you will be alright inside if I keep the door open?" Nell asks. Holly swallows and nods. Hesitant as it is, it is an affirmation that Nell accepts, and she pushes the door open.

Holly steps inside, and Nell follows only far enough to hold the door open with her body. She watches Holly move further into the room, staying within the thin, dim sliver of light that the hallway casts into the room. Holly stops right as the light tapers off, and then she turns around.

CLXXVIII

"What is this room for?" Holly asks, her voice small but curious. Nell attributes the former to her anxiety at being locked inside in the dark once more, and smiles.

"This is where we will save your friends, Holly." Nell explains. "Soon, the rest of our people will bring in candles and solar lights that have gained power over the past weeks of summer, and we will light this hall up ready for their Saving Ceremony."

Holly spins around in a slow circle, taking in what little detail she can make out in the still relative darkness. Maybe she is imagining what it will look like with all the decorations Nell has described. When she has made a full rotation, she looks back to Nell. Nell thinks she can see a glimmer of fear in her eyes, but it is too dim and she is too far away for any distinguishable features to be made out. It could just as easily be surprise, or excitement, her eyebrows raised and an unsure glimmer in her eyes. Half of Holly's face is bathed in the light from the hall, while the other half has been shrouded in darkness.

Nell holds out a hand, and Holly begins walking towards her. "Would you like to help us set everything up?" Holly hesitates and looks into Nell's eyes when she reaches the door. Whatever Nell thinks she might have seen in those doe-brown eyes is gone, replaced with a soft reverence that warms Nell's heart to the core.

Holly smiles. "I would love to." Then she shifts her gaze away from Nell's, before sliding it back up. "Though, I have a question first."

Nell nods. "Of course. Ask your question, Holly."

"Where did you put all our things when you captured us?" Holly asks quietly. They are back in the hallway now, the door to the dark hall closed behind them, the darkness that exists beyond the doors forgotten for now.

"Why do you ask that?" Nell frowns. Tilts her head. Holly scratches one arm with her blood-stained fingernails.

"My watch," she says, and swallows as she shrugs. "It was a gift from my father. He died when I was very young. It's all I have left of him, and if it's possible, I'd like it back." Holly looks up at Nell then, a kind of shame in her eyes. At asking for something so sentimental. At admitting something so personal about her past.

Nell considers the request. Because it is a request, not a question. Holly does not care about the rest of the confiscated goods. She does not care about the guns and the torchlights and the navigation devices that Nell's people took off Renee and her friends when they were captured. Holly only cares about her father's watch, and as she considers this, Nell smiles.

"Of course," she says, voice soft, kind. Holly's eyes light up. "I must help begin the preparations, help bring everything over to the hall. But I can have Emory take you to where your things are being kept. She can help you find your watch."

"Thank you, Nell," Holly says, a smile spreading across her lips. "Thank you."

THIRTY FIVE

Holly
Day 5
2280 C.E.

E mory is quiet as she leads Holly through the halls. That suits Holly just fine, as she is becoming accustomed with the space now, learning the maze of corridors and memorising them as best she can so she can lead her friends out of here later.

Nell had been so willing to let Holly have her watch back. She had not even considered that Holly would attempt to betray her, that she would steal back her group's guns and torchlights and navigational devices and escape into the night with them in hand and her group in tow. Holly considers, as Emory leads her to the stash of confiscated goods, what she will do when they return home. She wants, deep in her heart, to go straight to Sammy, to break him free of whatever mental block is forced upon their brains when one of the scientists' minds are implanted into their own. Holly wracks her brain for the name of the scientist in Sammy's head, and comes up empty. It is not like it matters, anyway. He is irrelevant to her cause; Sammy is the only one who matters. Their mother is gone — their father died long ago.

But then Holly considers whether she should even let anyone know that she is, in fact, Holly, and not Renee. Would she be safer if she admitted the truth, if she told the Bunkers what happens to a host's mind once they are infected with a scientist's? Or would they not care about the ethical conundrum of it all, of having trapped hundreds of innocents over the centuries without knowing about it?

Holly wonders if they have known the whole time that this is what happens when they infect a mind with their own, and casts that thought aside, because the reactions of her companions here in the cultists' commune suggests otherwise. They had been shocked to learn that it was even possible for the host's mind to return to them; they would not have been so surprised if they had known that Holly's consciousness was lurking in the shadows for over a year, watching and experiencing everything Renee Clarke had.

Perhaps she can convince one of the scientists to reverse-engineer what they do to Bunkers' minds. Perhaps one of the more reasonable ones, perhaps Flora — *Sylvia* — or Jerry — *Mickey* — would be willing to at least hear her out, listen to her rambling arguments. It is a long shot, but she is more than willing to put her own life on the line if it will save countless generations.

She just needs to speak with Sammy, first.

Her brother was seventeen when Holly was infected with Renee Clarke. It has been more than a year now, so he has been infected with whichever scientist he belongs to genealogically — they are passed down through family lines, after all. It is how Holly and her mother both were turned into Renee Clarke upon their eighteenth birthdays.

Emory comes to a stop by a door on the second floor of the building, where two cultists stand guard outside. She takes out a ring of keys from her pants' pocket, and fiddles with it for a few seconds to find the right one. Holly watches the guards out of the corner of her eye, but neither of them move. They do not even flinch. It is as if they are made of stone, turned to statues as punishment for their crimes. But Holly knows — though she does not know how — that they will spring into action if she makes any sudden or suspicious movements. So she trains her gaze ahead and waits for Emory to let her into this room.

It is dark inside, but there is a window on the far side of the room that at least a little natural light can sneak in through. It is still raining, so the light is dim, but it is enough to move around the room by, and Holly follows Emory into the belly of the beast.

Emory says, "Find your watch," and something like a shock of electricity sparks up Holly's body. It is an order. This she understands perfectly well. And her body begins to move of its own volition, sliding her feet across the floor to the first wooden crate of things on her left. She sorts through the items, useless knickknacks that do not belong to Holly or her companions, then the second crate, with items of clothing that she does not know where they got, but does not want to ask. Holly had seen, as soon as she entered the room, that the guns are somewhere on the right of the room, so she just has to do a terrible job of looking through these crates for her watch so that she can get around to the other side of the room.

She finds the navigational devices before anything else, and skims over them briefly, moving to the next crate along. From this new angle, Holly can see Emory more clearly, can see where her gaze is trained on the floor at her feet. With a racing heart, Holly turns back to the crate with the navigational devices and quickly pockets one, careful not to make too many quick movements.

She lets out a long breath and hopes it is not as shaky as her fingers feel as she digs her hands back into the crate in front of her.

"Have you found it yet?" Emory asks. Holly swallows against the lump in her throat and turns to look at her.

"No," Holly says, and shakes her head. Emory does not say anything in response to that, only continues to stare her down, so Holly turns back to the task at hand. On the sixth crate, her fingers finally catch on something leather, and Holly stills her movements. This is it, then.

She has not managed to work all the way around to the guns, and she is sure Emory will order her out of the room as soon as she produces the watch from the crate. She has fulfilled the task; she has found her watch. But Emory did not say anything about what to do when she finds it. She did not say what to do next. So Holly lets go of the watch's strap and continues onto the next crate.

The guns are almost in reach, now. This is the last crate before the wall where they have been lined up like soldiers standing at attention. Their sleek, black bodies catch the little light streaming in through the window, and Holly is almost drawn to them like a moth to flame. But she remains focused on the crate before her, and sorts through it with a — by now — practiced slow intensity. She makes sure she does not work any faster or slower than she had any of the previous crates. She does not want to arouse any suspicion in Emory, not this close to her goal.

"Wait," Emory says, and Holly is helpless to the way the seizing of her muscles brings all her movements to a stop. Her heartbeat skips and races as panic builds in her chest and spreads out through the rest of her body.

Emory steps away from the post she had taken up by the door and Holly cannot track her movements across the room with anything but the sound of footsteps reaching her ears. She cannot turn her head, cannot even dart her eyes to a place where she would be able to see Emory's advances. Emory moves slowly, and quietly, and the room is silent but for their breaths and Emory's heavy boots on the linoleum.

There is some quiet rustling around in one of the crates, and then Emory says, "Is this your watch?" She holds up a watch in front of Holly's face, and Holly can only blink. It is her watch. Its worn leather strap and chipped glass face. Its golden casing and black hands on a white face. It is the watch Holly — and then Renee — has worn every day since she was seven and her mother had come home crying, telling her and Sammy that their father is dead and this is all that is left of him.

"Yes," Holly manages to say at last. She is still stuck to the spot, like a tree whose roots have taken hold. "I guess I skipped over it on accident. Thank you," she adds afterward, straining her eyes to look over at Emory. Her face is impassive, perfectly blank. It is infuriating, because Holly cannot, for the life of her, work out what Emory is thinking. It is terrifying, because she could have caught on to Holly's plan, and Holly would not know it.

But then Emory says, "Relax," and hands over the watch when Holly's shoulders sag and she reaches for it. She says nothing more, and turns for the door. Holly looks down at the watch in her hands, flips it over to read the engraving on the back: *Believe you can.* She'd once asked her father what that simple message really means, and he had told her that she will understand when the time comes. Holly rubs a grimy, bloody thumb over the text, then grips the watch in one hand and takes in a deep breath. She flicks her gaze to Emory, heading for the door, and she finally understands the watch's message.

Believe you can.

Holly believes she can make it home.

She lunges for the nearest gun.

THIRTY SIX

Nell
12 Weeks
199 P.A.

G unshots ring loud as Nell hangs up a string of solar lights in the hall. She turns, same as everyone else, and comes to a realisation that she should have made hours ago, days ago, years ago: It is impossible to get through to a Renee Clarke about her cause. It appears that it does not matter if it is Renee herself, or the body she is inhabiting.

Nell is a fool to have ever tried.

CXC

But was she not simply following her predecessors? Was she not simply following the words and instructions of Willow? Of Ambrose? Of Nerissa and Orlando? Their writings had been so clear, so straightforward, that Nell had believed any doubters of the goal to be the fools.

If it is possible to cut through to Renee Clarke, the others will soon follow. Bunkers are nothing if not sheep in wolves' clothing, as the saying goes: They act as though they are capable of individual thought, but I have observed nothing but the opposite. They flock around Renee Clarke as if she is the sheepdog tasked with keeping them safe from harm, safe from the true wolves out there. Safe from us.

"Everyone, stay close to the walls, and close the doors after me." Nell says. She gestures for Constance and Guy to follow after her, and makes for the door on the other side of the hall.

The three of them hurry down the corridor and back to the atrium. They glance around, listening for more gunshots, but there are none. Nell jerks her head one way and gestures for Constance and Guy to follow her. They take the stairs up to the second floor, and move slowly along the hallway, on guard for any fast movements in their direction.

CXCI

They round corners slowly, and take count of any out of the ordinary sounds that might be Holly. A gunshot sounds, too close for comfort, and they press themselves up against a wall, holding their breaths and keeping as quiet as they possibly can. "I don't want to hurt any of you," Holly says, her voice shaky and echoey a little as it spirals down the hallway to reach Nell's ears. "I just want to go home. Just let me go home."

A few seconds of quiet, of unsteady calm, and then there is the squeak of a shoe against the floor, closer than Holly's voice had been only moments ago, but from the opposite direction. A flicker of dark hair out of the corner of Nell's eye, and she spins around to look at it head-on. There, Holly stands, just around the corner in another hallway. A gun in her hand, she raises it and levels it right at Nell's head.

"Stop!" Constance shouts, but she forgets, in a community where many have the gift, that she does not. She is not descended of the Originals. She cannot tell Holly what to do right now with only the power of her voice. Guy can, but he has not yet rounded the corner to see Holly standing there.

Holly does not hesitate in pulling the trigger. A loud pop echoes around the corridors. Nell's heartbeat stutters.

But it goes wide, misses her by a few inches, and Nell heaves a deep breath in. "Stop," she says on the out-breath, and Holly freezes in place. Gun still raised, aim still focused on Nell. Nell's heart stutters once more, and then she stumbles forward a step, toward Holly.

Holly cannot move, cannot speak. As Nell approaches, she knows she is no longer in danger, but there is a reason her community has never really used the automatic weapons they take from those they save: They are unpredictable at best, deadly in the wrong hands. And right now, Holly is the wrong hands for this gun to be in.

Nell walks over and stands right next to Holly. Right up next to her face, crowding into her space. Holly's eyes dart to the side, wide and shocked, like she forgot that Nell could have this power over her with no more than one simple word.

"I had such faith in you, Holly," Nell shakes her head, her tone disappointed. "How could you betray your people like this? Betray *me* like this?" She shakes her head again and sighs, then turns back to Constance and Guy, who linger a few metres away.

CXCIII

"Collect the others. Take them to the hall." Nell says. Then, looking Holly in the eye once more, says, "I will handle Holly Mason." It is not a threat. Nell would never threaten Holly, not even now, when she has committed such an act of betrayal, of borderline treason, in attempting to kill Nell and escape. No. Nell would never dream of hurting Holly.

Constance and Guy's footsteps disappear down the hall, back the way they came, and Nell waits until she cannot hear them any longer to say, "Give me the gun, Holly." Holly obeys, because she must, because she has no other choice. She holds it out, grip on it loose enough that Nell can simply pluck it out of her hands with very little resistance. Holly's breath comes in quick, sharp bursts as worry takes over. She eyes the gun, now in Nell's hands, and tears begin to well up in her eyes.

"Did you kill Emory?" Nell asks, handling the gun with such care that it might as well be the most fragile thing she has ever held. Holly does not answer. It is a question, not a command, after all. She must have worked out the intricacies and loopholes of Nell's ability to force compliance, then. Nell tilts her head.

She rephrases the query: "Tell me if Emory is dead." And this time, Holly opens her mouth, answers.

"Yes," she says, voice small and wavering. Her eyes flicker from the gun to Nell's face, and then back again, as if only a single second without her attention glued to its rough, black frame is enough time for Nell to hold it up to Holly's face and shoot her right through the brain. But Nell is not so barbaric. She is not so kind, either: When Holly Mason dies, it will be slowly, and painfully, and Nell will enjoy every second of it.

Nell hums. "Tell me why you killed her." This is strange, ordering Holly to answer her. With Renee Clarke, Nell only ever needed to ask, and she would comply, and she had thought the same might be true of Holly Mason, as well. Clearly she was wrong.

"She would have stopped me," Holly says. The words come out clunky, like she doesn't want to be speaking. But she has to. She has no other choice, not when Nell has commanded it. Nell relishes in the feeling of authority that washes over her at this thought, at the thought that she, alone, has control over Holly's actions in this moment. She could command Holly to take back the gun and shoot herself in the head, and she would have no other choice but to comply.

But Nell blinks and takes a step back, because that is not what she wants. It is not what she wants to do. It is not what she will do.

Holly mistakes this stepping back as Nell being shocked at her reason for killing Emory, and says, "It was quick. I made sure it was quick. She didn't suffer long. At least I can say it was merciful — can you?"

A hatred flares up in Nell's gut at that.

At *least I can say it was merciful — can you?*

"We save people here, Holly," Nell says, slow, calculated, low so that she does not shout. "We save them. We do not kill for no reason. What we do is mercy. We are saving people from this horrid existence, allowing them to experience peace and tranquillity in whatever life awaits us after this one."

"But what if there's nothing?" Holly asks, a little frantic, words coming out no louder than a breath. "What if there's nothing after we die, and you've been wrong this whole time? What if you've just been killing innocent people this whole time?"

"If there is nothing but the void after we die," Nell says and raises her chin. "Then at least it will be calm. I cannot say the same for this world we live in now."

Nell takes in a deep breath, looks Holly up and down where she is still frozen to the spot but for her eyes and her lips. "Sleep," she says, and Holly collapses the floor, unconscious at once.

THIRTY SEVEN

Renee
3 Days
2280 C.E.

Would it really be so bad? If they killed us all? We're no better than the team that started all this. No better than their experiments.

At least ours worked.

At least we didn't end the world with our research.

But would it really be so bad? No one in the bunker but Isadora knows about the lapse in my memory. It's an *uncontrolled variable, sure, but at least it's not one they're wilfully ignoring.*

Who will my memory go to next? I don't have any more descendants after Holly. Maybe they'll pass it on to Siobhan. She's lined up to take Clio, but she has a sister who can do that job. Or maybe I'll go to the sister.

At least, if they put me in someone else, no one alive but Isadora will ever know about the gap in my memory.

And I think I can live with that.

But would it be so bad to be gone for good?

THIRTY EIGHT

Holly
Day 5
2280 C.E.

H olly's head pounds like a drum as she comes to. It is a heavy, thumping thing, the headache that blooms behind her eyelids and in her forehead.

She groans and moves her hand up to her face to rub at her forehead, an attempt to relieve some of the stress there.

At least, she tries to.

CC

She opens her eyes and looks down to her sides, which her arms are pinned to with thick, fraying ropes. Holly's heartrate picks up as she begins to panic and struggle against the restraints. Her head thumps back onto the wall behind her and Holly squeezes her eye shut again as she lets out a pained breath.

"Please stop fighting, Holly."

Holly freezes at that voice and looks up once more. Nell has come to stand right in front of her, her head tilted to one side and her eyes searching. Scanning over Holly's face for something that Holly cannot quite place. She is not sure what, exactly, Nell is looking for. But she cannot look away from Nell as she looks her fill, because there is a beauty to her that Holly has never noticed before now. She was telling the truth, at least, when she said the hall would be lit up *Like a Christmas tree*, because behind and all around Nell are hanging strings of solar lights casting a soft, warm, yellow glow on her from all sides. Her eyelashes look longer, and her chestnut-brown hair seems smoother, almost like all of the dirt and grease and grime has been washed and brushed out of it. Her cheeks are rosy, and her eyes sparkle with something Holly can only think to describe as pure, unfiltered joy. Ecstasy, though Holly only knows about the drug from the books she read in her childhood. It is both mesmerising and horrifying, and Holly cannot draw her gaze away from Nell's.

"Please don't do this," Holly's voice wobbles as she stops struggling against the vines. "You don't have to do this. I'll stay. I promise. Just please, don't kill me." She considers, for a moment, offering that Nell sever her Achilles tendon, leave her incapable of running away, but then supposes that Nell would consider her a useless and inadequate addition to her community if she cannot even stand on her own two feet.

"You could have stood by my side, Holly," Nell says, her voice soft, and low, only for Holly to hear. It is disappointed, but not frustrated, at Holly's actions. "We could have done this together, saved your friends together." She clicks her tongue and shakes her head. "But now look at what you have done. You have given me no other choice. Your friends *will* be saved today; you will die, too, but you will not be saved."

Nell looks to her left, and Holly copies the movement. At her right, across the hall, sit Sandra, and Irene, and Lee, and Nikolai. They are all awake, all looking over at Holly and Nell. Holly can hardly make out the expressions on their faces this far away and in the dim lighting, but she is sure there is something like fear in their eyes, something like horror in their hearts. She feels the same, is sure their expressions are mirrored on her own face. Holly feels the sudden urge to break free of her restraints and run over to them, to hold them all close and promise that they will get through this together, alive, and that they will make it home, safe. But she knows it is not the truth, that they will all die here, unless, by some miracle, their friends in the bunker have managed to pinpoint the cultists' location and actually make it here, rather than get shot down on their own home turf. Holly hopes they have, hopes they are about to burst through the doors across the hall with the big, green sign that Holly guesses once claimed it to be an exit. She wishes she could make a break for it through those doors, but the ropes keeping her pressed up against the wall bring her back to the reality that Nell has laid out so perfectly for her: *You will die, too, but you will not be saved.*

This is the end of the line for Holly.

She thinks, in this moment, of Renee. She does not know why, because Renee was never anything but a promised honour and a living nightmare, but Holly seeks her out, dives into the deep recesses of her mind to try and find where Renee's consciousness has gone. What would Renee think in this moment? What would she say? Holly could never read Renee's thoughts, not even when she was trapped inside her own mind, but she found, quite quickly, that she could guess at what Renee might say or do in reaction to certain situations. She had, after all, spent so many years with her in the form of her own mother. It was so, so easy to determine her reactions to things when she realised she was still dealing with her mother.

Holly decides that in this moment, Renee would throw a fit. She would scream, and thrash about, trying beyond all hope to break free of her restraints. She would refuse to give up the fight until she physically could hold out no longer. Holly decides that in this moment, Renee would argue with Nell, would yell obscenities at her, and mock her beliefs.

But Holly will do none of these things. Because she is not Renee. She has never wanted to be a killer, but the circumstances she had found herself in an hour ago — two? Three? Longer? She is not sure how long she was passed out — had forced her hand. Had made her a killer. She blinks, and she sees Emory, grasping at her chest, and then at her thigh, and then falling to the ground, motionless, no longer breathing. She blinks again, and imagines Nell doing the same, and is overcome with a wave of nausea at the thought.

A loud, ear-splitting crack and rumbling roll of thunder snap Holly out of her soon-meaningless train of thought, and she looks, once more, at Nell. She has moved away from Holly now, and is walking over to the stage to Holly's left. Holly had not noticed them before, but it appears that every member of Nell's community is here in the hall, too. They have crowded by the stage, standing in a single, curved line spanning from one end of the stage to the other. Holly is briefly taken aback; she had not realised there were so many people living here.

"Friends," Nell says as she approaches the line of people, who are all dressed in the same soot-coloured, floor-length robes that Nell is. Her voice echoes around the mostly empty space, and Holly feels a little more nauseous as she finally fully comprehends what is about to happen: She is going to have to watch her friends be killed — *sacrificed* — before being killed herself. Cold, salty tears fall onto her cheeks and she does not bother trying to blink them back.

Nell reaches the stage and turns around, so that every member of her community can see her. And so can Holly, if she strains her neck and allows that headache to pulse harder, stronger, behind her eyes. "We have gathered here today to celebrate the saving of four souls." Nell announces. She smiles at the group gathered in front of her, like they truly are her best friends, like they have come to watch a performance, rather than a ritual sacrifice to the insane beliefs they all share.

The thing is, though, that Holly thinks she understands some of their insane beliefs. She has not had much time, has not spent all that long with these people, learning what they believe. But what Nell has explained, especially about death and their beliefs around what happens to a person once they die, is something that Holly can understand. She can see how these people cling to such a belief system, even if she does not understand the complex and intricate beliefs of the faith.

So it is not so insane, then, is it, if she can understand some of the reasoning behind what they are doing? This does not mean that Holly condones the murder that brings about the forever-happiness Nell has spoken of, especially when there is no proof of such a thing after death. God, Renee's scientific reasoning is infecting her mind.

The truth is that Nell and the rest of these people have no clue what happens to a person after they die, and they are only hoping that their belief is the right one, because if it is not, then they are killing innocents for no reason other than that they think they know what will happen.

We have gathered here today to celebrate the saving of four souls, Nell says, but what she really means is this: *We have gathered here today to slaughter four innocent people.* Eight, really, but Holly doubts that Nell — or any of the people surrounding her, praising her and the community she and her ancestors have built around such lies and blind faith — cares about the people trapped inside their own minds and bodies. She doubts that Nell considers them little more than insignificant inconveniences, and wonders if the only reason that she cares about Holly at all is because she surfaced, forced Renee back into the recesses of her mind. Because suddenly Holly was more interesting than the body-snatching, parasitic scientist who had taken over her body and life.

"Bring forth our first lucky soul." Nell says, and extends an arm through the slight gap between two people in front of her, and the two on each inner end of the semi-circle break off and turn towards Holly's friends at the other end of the hall. Holly tracks their movements with her eyes, and when they go to Irene first, her breath gets caught in her throat. She has never liked Irene; she hates her, even. But to think that this is how she will die is just plain *wrong*. She does not deserve to die like this. And even though it is also Aoife dying, it is not, really. She will simply be implanted into another unlucky Bunker's brain. Irene does not have any sisters, so perhaps the parasite will go to Ellie, or Annalise, who are almost eighteen. The thought alone makes Holly feel as though she is going to throw up. She clamps her jaw together and swallows down the bile.

"No," Irene says, and Holly only just catches the sound of it. "No," she says, louder this time, and then, "No! No! Get away from me! Get your hands off me! No!" She scrambles back on the wooden floor, but her hands are tied together behind her back, so she does not get far enough fast enough, and then the cultists' hands are on her, dragging her to her feet. They pull her, kicking and screaming, towards the rest of their group, and Holly watches, incapable of helping from her position, only able to watch, to look upon the scene like it is a film, as the cultists' drag Irene all the way past their semi-circle of like-mindedly deranged individuals and to Nell.

They kick in the backs of Irene's knees and force her to the ground unceremoniously. Holly cannot hear the sound of her kneecaps hitting the wood over the sound of her protesting screams that are quickly going hoarse. The sheer volume of her shrieks alone has Holly's ears splitting down the middle like a piece of firewood.

"No! Please! I'll do anything!" Irene's screams turn to sobs, and she lets her head loll down, as if she is awaiting the executioner's cleaver coming down on the back of her neck. But Nell only looks down at her with the most serene expression on her face that Holly has ever seen. It is a little startling, considering in the days Holly has spent with her, Nell has almost only ever been calm and collected; but this is a whole other level of insane, because if she can look upon someone so afraid to die, someone who does not want to be 'saved,' then what does that truly say about Nell?

That she is just as unhinged as Renee claimed she was at the beginning of this horror show.

"There is nothing you can do to change your fate now," Nell says, shaking her head. "You should be thankful. We are saving you. Now, what is your name?"

"Fuck you!" Irene shouts at her. "Fuck you! You're all insane!"

"What is your name?" Nell persists, even in the face of such abject dismissal. Irene continues to shout obscenities in Nell's face, so Nell turns her eyes away from her and to the group surrounding her.

Someone says, "It's Aoife," and Nell tilts her head at them, her lips pursed.

"No," she says. "Her real name? Did she tell you?"

"Why the fuck would I tell any of you that?" Irene spits, and she starts to laugh in Nell's face. Nell does not look back at her, but instead over at Holly, and Holly's skin breaks out in a cold sweat all over at that piercing gaze. She feels like a prey animal who has been spotted by a predator; Nell will lunge at her rip open her throat at the first opportunity.

"Holly," Nell says, and Holly cannot really hear the sound of her own name on Nell's lips, not from so far away and with Irene's laughter echoing around the hall, but she can see the way Nell's mouth moves to form the two syllable word.

Holly begins hyperventilating, her breaths coming in quick and shallow, and she cannot look away from Nell's face as she raises an expectant eyebrow. Another clap of thunder, and Holly goes stick-straight against the wall.

She does not want to tell Nell Irene's name. She does not want to give that away. No matter that she so strongly dislikes her, no matter that, in their childhood, she would have gladly told Nell Irene's name. But giving it to her here, now, would be a death sentence for Irene, more than she already has, knelt before Nell, waiting for the final blow. It would be desecration of something so sacred as a name, the first gift a child is presented with. Holly may hate Irene; but she will not betray her like this, and knows if their positions were reversed, Irene would do the same.

Holly shakes her head. Nell narrows her eyes. Holly clamps her jaw shut. Nell purses her lips.

"Tell me what your name is." Nell says, looking back down at Irene, and the name comes from her mouth with no more resistance than water flowing down an unobstructed stream. As soon as she says her own name, Irene is wailing again, shouting that it is not true, that she lied. But everyone in the hall knows that cannot be the truth. Because Nell and who knows how many others in that group all clustered up by the stage can make anyone do anything they want with the power of a single word. Nell could make Irene take a knife and gut herself, stab herself in the stomach over and over and over again until she collapses from the blood loss and keep going until the light drains from her eyes and the colour from her face and the blood entirely from her body. Until she is nothing but an empty husk of the person — people — she once was, bleeding out on the wood at Nell's feet.

And she just might, because now Nell is walking to the stage and taking a knife with an elaborately decorated handle up from the collection spread out in front of her. She brings it over to Irene, where she has stopped struggling against the cultists' grips on her shoulders, likely because they have ordered her to do so, and holds it out towards her, blade first.

"Irene," Nell says, and the name is sour coming from her mouth. As soon as she says it, Holly looks at Irene and no longer sees her as such. She cannot, for the sake of keeping the scientist inside her and the person she truly is separate. Holly must now see them as two physically separate entities, like Aoife is Irene's identical sister, and Irene is somewhere else, somewhere safe, far away from here.

So Holly looks not upon Irene, but upon Aoife, and as she listens to her continue to scream at Nell, drowning out whatever Nell is saying to her, Holly imagines a world in which she and Irene had been friends. Maybe it exists. Maybe it could have, if the bunker had not been so hell-bent on competition, even when it really amounted to nothing in the end. She considers whether that reality, where they are friends, can still exist. Whether, if the cultists are right, and Irene — not Aoife, never Aoife — really will go onto some other plane of existence after death, she will have the chance to experience that friendship. Holly considers this, and feels the corners of her lips tug upwards. Perhaps it is not so bad, after all, what Nell and the cultists believe. Perhaps believing such a thing can bring Holly some peace of mind, can soothe her regrets about never befriending Irene when she had the chance.

Perhaps, if Holly can convince Nell that she truly does believe such a thing, that she truly is willing to believe some more, then Nell will let her live.

THIRTY NINE

Nell
11 Weeks
199 P.A.

T he squelch of Irene's blood under her skin
bubbles out and onto Nell's hand where she
holds the knife in her chest all the way up to the
handle.

Irene's eyes go wide and she gasps in a crackly
breath. Nell lets go of the knife and steps back. With her
bloody thumb, Nell presses a single line into the centre of
Irene's forehead. Irene chokes on her blood and some of

it comes up and out of her mouth, spilling over her chin and dribbling onto the wood before her like a baby who cannot keep their food down. She begins to tilt forward, but Constance and Freya behind her grip a shoulder each and keep her upright.

Nell steps back to the altar and collects the second knife. As she walks back to Irene, Holly cries out. "You've already killed her," she says. "You don't need to do any more. Just leave her. Don't draw this out, Nell." And Nell looks over to Holly briefly, confused as to why she thinks she has any say in how this goes. Holly does not know the ins and outs of this ritual, of this ceremony. She did not open herself to learning about Nell and her people's beliefs.

"Do not tell me how to do this," Nell tells her, lifting her chin to look at Holly over the tops of her people's heads. "I have been doing this longer than you had Renee Clarke inside of your head. I know what I am doing, and I will not compromise this saving ceremony because you think you have the right to tell me what to do."

"Nell, this is ridiculous!" Holly shouts. A flare of anger rises in Nell's gut.

"Be quiet!" Nell yells back, and Holly's mouth clamps shut. Nell takes a few long, deep breaths, and turns back to Irene. She is slumped forward even further now, and the looks on Constance and Freya's faces suggests that it is a struggle to hold her up. Nell does not have long to complete the ceremony before Irene dies without having been saved. She must hurry.

Bright, white light momentarily blinds Nell, and is followed, after a few seconds, by a deafening crack of thunder. "Irene, may you find salvation. May you pass on from this life and find peace and safety in the next. May life be kinder to you there than it ever was here." Freya slides her hand into Irene's hair and curls her fingers into a fist to pull her head back up so that she is looking at Nell. She would be, anyhow, if her eyelids had not slid shut. Nell's heartbeat picks up out of worry that Irene's has stopped, and she leans forward, quickly slicing a deep line from one side of Irene's throat to the other. Thick, viscous, red blood pours from the wound and joins the rest of the liquid in trickling down Irene's chest and torso, down her legs and pooling on the wooden floorboards beneath her knees.

Out of the corner of her eye, Nell can see Holly thrash about in her restraints, desperate to break free but unable to do so. Nell does not pay her any attention, though, keeping her gaze instead focused wholly on

Irene's heavy body as Constance and Freya pull at her limbs and drag her up to the altar, where they position her just so, with her arms spread out to her sides and bent at the elbow so that her forearms point down towards her feet. And then, when they are finished, Nell nods, and gestures for Constance and Freya to bring over the next individual to be saved.

As Constance takes the first step down off the altar to follow the silent command, another blinding moment of light takes over the room, and an almost immediate crack of thunder follows. Screams sound off from all around Nell, but she can barely hear them. The booming sound echoes around inside her skull as if it is hollow, and she is thrown off her feet, landing squarely on her back. The breath is squeezed out of her lungs. Her skull cracks on the wooden floorboards, and Nell's vision goes static for a brief moment. When she opens her eyes, her vision is blurry, but there is a bright orange glow not far in front of her, and it is suddenly so warm in the hall.

No. It is not supposed to be here yet.

We still have eleven weeks.

We are supposed to have more time.

Someone's hand comes up under Nell's arm and hauls her to her feet, but all the bones in her legs have disappeared, and she cannot stand on her own two feet for longer than a second before collapsing to the ground once more. A stabbing pain shoots up her back from her ass, and Nell cries out in pain. At least, she thinks she does. She still cannot hear anything but a ringing in her ears so deafening no other sound breaks the barrier.

And then a shrill, mocking laughter breaks through. Nell whips her head around, never mind the jarring headache that blooms at once behind her eyes and at her temples. Never mind that the spell of dizziness that overwhelms her is almost as debilitating as the silence had been only moments prior. Something is getting through to her, and Nell must find its source.

Is it the entity who is bringing about this apocalypse, come to mock her and her ancestors for ever believing they could fight it off with their sacrifices? Have they come back with a vengeance, more determined than they were two hundred years ago to wipe out the human race once and for all? Is this truly the end for Nell, no matter that she has dedicated her entire life to preventing the second end of the world? The *proper* end of the world?

"You're all fucking idiots! You've always been so fucking stupid!" And no, that is not the voice of some ancient god who has the power to destroy the earth so easily, so carelessly. That is the voice of a girl who has been made quiet, who should still be silent, even as everything falls apart around her.

Nell struggles to her feet and looks around, more thoroughly this time. And she spots her: Over by the wall that she had been tied to, now stumbling away from it as the ends of the rope have snapped and set her free, is Holly Mason. A grin spreads across her face, so wide, so unbalanced, that Nell is, for the first time in her life, terrified of another human being. It would be curious, if it were not so bone-chilling, that someone can laugh in the face of destruction, that Holly can look the end of her life in the eye and smile. It would be curious, if it were not so horrifying, that this is the only time, ever, that Nell has registered fear as an emotion coursing through her veins. Not at the hall crumbling around her; not even at the inevitable end to her life and the planet as a whole — but at Holly's expression, and the carelessness with which she now speaks of the situation at hand.

And then Nell realises that this cannot be Holly. Oh, how she wishes it was. She wishes that this was scared, wide-eyed, curious Holly Mason that Nell is looking upon. But she knows how her ability to control others' works, and Nell never said that Holly could speak again — but she never suggested that Renee Clarke should ever stop.

"No," Nell breathes, because she can still barely speak. "It is not possible." But is it not? How did Holly resurface to begin with? Why would it be so unreasonable to believe that Renee could figure out how to do the same?

There is the unmistakable groan of something heavy, and Nell looks up just in time to see a sheet of roofing by the altar break away and begin falling towards the floor. It is on fire, and as it smacks down with a thunderous clap, sparks fly out in every direction. A few land scattered not far from where Nell stands, and she jumps back when some collide with the sleeve of her robe. The remnants of the fire start eating away at the thin fabric at once, and Nell yelps as she tries to put it out.

But she does not have long to dwell on the fact that she is on fire, because then she is being tackled to the ground.

"I'll fucking kill you!" Renee yells as she climbs on top of Nell. She brings back her arm and slams her fist into the side of Nell's face, a resounding crack sending Nell's head rolling to the side as all thoughts scramble in her brain.

You cannot, Nell thinks. It is the only thing she *can* think as Renee continues pummelling her face with her fist. *You cannot kill me.*

But that will not stop her from trying.

FORTY

Renee
Day 1
2280 C.E.

Nell's cheek splitting under Renee's knuckles feels so good she could scream.

She hits Nell, over and over and over again, and savours the ache of her own flesh bursting at the seams, the feel of her own blood, slick against her skin, mingling with Nell's. And Nell doesn't fight back, and Renee feels a little sick at that, at the fact that this isn't a fair fight. But she doesn't care. Nell has had this coming, and even if Renee still can't step over the edge, still can't kill her, then at least the burning building will finish off this job for her.

But she doesn't want it to. Renee wants to be the one to end Nell, to end this all, even at the cost of her own life. Because nothing matters anymore, does it? Maybe Nell's been right all along. Maybe this is the second apocalypse. Maybe they will actually all be wiped out this time. But Renee can't bring herself to care. Not anymore. And it feels so freeing to just not care. And as Renee brings her fist back once more, slams it into Nell's nose once more, reels from the punch as the vibrations slide up her arm and into her shoulder blades once more, she feels herself start to laugh.

It's a strange sensation, this laughter. It bubbles up in her chest, gets stuck in her throat, and goes nowhere in the end. It comes out sounding choked — not that Renee can really hear it over the shrieking of everyone around them, running about like headless chickens and trying to escape the fire. But Renee doesn't care about them, just like she doesn't care about her own wellbeing. She's single-mindedly focused on one goal; kill Nell.

"This is your fault!" She screams, her voice going raw. "This is your fucking fault! You could've just let us go! You could've just let us live!" But Nell doesn't respond. Renee doesn't give her the chance to, throwing fists into her cheeks, her eyes, her jaw. She even sends one perfectly aimed hit at Nell's throat, and Nell coughs and chokes at that. Renee feels a sick little thrill spark somewhere deep in her gut at the curdled sounds.

When she's tired herself out, when she's confident Nell won't take the first opportunity she gets to lash out and hit Renee, Renee finally sits back on her heels, straddling Nell, and takes in big gulps of air, feeling it travel down her trachea to her lungs. It rips her open from the inside, as if the air is suddenly poisonous, and when Renee drags her eyes away from Nell she sees the burning stage across the room, the tattered curtains up in flame, and remembers that oh, that's smoke she's inhaling.

Renee looks around the hall and spots many of Nell's people crowded around the emergency exit, its broken green plastic sign mocking their inability to get the door open. Many more of them are simply bodies, littered across the hall's floor, lying dead from the lightning strike that Renee thinks is what allowed her to jump back into the controls of Holly's body. But she's not going to question it. She's back, and she's going to kill Nell.

CCXXIV

Renee gets to her feet, shaky and unstable, and as she does, another sheet of roofing breaks away and falls to the floor with a resounding smack. It shakes the floor, and Renee almost falls back onto Nell, but manages to keep steady. She looks back down at Nell, desperate to make sure she's still there, still just as helpless and broken and bloodied as she was when Renee stood up.

Then she stumbles off, slowly, because in that first shockwave, that first lightning strike that set the auditorium ablaze, Renee knocked the back of her head so hard into the wall behind her that she swears she heard a crack, and now every time she takes a step, her vision gets a little bit blurrier, her hearing gets a little bit fuzzier, and her head gets a little bit heavier.

She swears she hears Holly screaming at her from within her own mind. But that might just be her subconscious, telling her that this is wrong, that she should stop trying to kill Nell and find a way out of this burning building before she gets herself killed instead. Either way, Renee ignores that little voice yelling at her and walks off toward the stage.

Everything's up in flames, from the once-red curtains framing the stage to what might once have been Aoife's body that is now being charred so unceremoniously that Renee's glad she died before she was burned. She almost wishes she were Aoife right now. At least she won't have to watch the world come crumbling down around her. At least she'll be able to wake up in the bunker never having known the pain she must have suffered in her last few minutes in this body. If this storm really is just a storm, if Nell and her people haven't been right about a second end of the world this whole time, then maybe Renee will be afforded the same liberties.

Something in her doubts it, though.

A wooden plank lays down beside Aoife's body, — Renee thinks that's Aoife, at least; it's difficult to tell, her being burnt to a crisp and all — and Renee bends to grab it. It's heavy in her hands, heavier than she'd expected. She drags it along behind her and stares intently at Nell's body as she makes her way slowly back over to her, focused on her destination, her goal, the last task for her to tick off in her mental to-do list.

Nell's coughing and sputtering when Renee approaches and stands over her. She looks up at Renee, doesn't even register the wooden plank she's clutching, and reaches a weak arm up towards her. Renee looks down at Nell, at her face, more bloodied than a face ought to be, and sneers. One of Nell's eyelids is swollen shut, and the other is halfway there. Her lips are split in at least two places, there's a gash along her cheekbone, and she's spitting up blood even as she looks up at Renee. Renee's surprised she hasn't choked on it yet.

"This is your fault," Renee says, only just loud enough that she thinks Nell can hear her. But maybe the thunder and lightning affected her hearing, or maybe she just doesn't want to say anything, because no words spill from her lips, only more blood. Renee heaves the plank of wood up to her shoulders and with as much force as she can muster, brings it down on Nell's torso. She hears ribs crack, break, and Nell's screaming so loud that it carries up and over all the other sounds in the hall — people still clambering for the door, people under heavy, burning chunks of the roof shouting for their friends to help them, the groans and cracks of an ancient building finally coming down.

Renee slides the plank of wood off of Nell, and Nell's hands wrap protectively around her ribs at once. She squeezes her eyes shut as cold tears slip from her eyes and mingle with the hot blood smeared across almost every inch of her face. Renee watches her groan in pain and feels that thrill build inside her, kindling to a flame in her gut that could rival the fiery inferno swallowing the hall whole. She brings the wood back up to her shoulders and goes to swing it down on Nell, but then there's a sharp, blinding pain in the back of her skull, and Renee cries out and drops the wood behind her as she falls to the floor. Her knees hit the wood hard, and reverberations pulse all the way up her thighs to her back. The shooting pain is there and gone again, but a lingering ache throbs at the back of her head. Renee brings a hand up to the spot, and presses gentle fingers to it, which she expects to send another wave of unbearable pain rushing through her body, but there isn't even the echoing remainders of an injury.

It must be Nell's twisted mind tricks, then, Renee reasons. She turns her gaze back to Nell, who's looking at her with that single half-open eye. Nell's lips split into a slow grin, and then she's laughing and crying out in pain in equal measure.

"You cannot kill me," she says through the hysteria, her voice raspy. The words gurgle in her throat as she chokes on her own blood.

"But I have," Renee says. "I may not be able to deal a finishing blow, but you are as good as dead. And I've done that. *Me.* No one else." She smiles down at Nell, a condescending thing. The hall is so hot around her, going up in flames no one has thought to even try and put out. Smoke clogs her airways, and she chokes on it as she tries to breathe in. Her head goes even foggier, but she blinks hard and focuses her gaze on Nell.

"You won't be able to kill anyone else anymore." Renee says. She swallows against her impossibly dry throat. "Because of *me*." But this must be the wrong thing to say, because then Nell's laughing louder, harder. She's gripping her torso even tighter, which will be doing nothing for the pain she must be in with all those broken ribs

"But this is not my fault. I did everything I could. I believed so hard for so long." Nell says, and Renee frowns and sneers at her. She coughs against the smoke swirling around in front of her.

"Then who's fault is it, Nell? Because from where I'm standing, it sure as fuck looks like it's yours."

Nell shakes her head, a slow, uncoordinated movement where her head just rocks back and forth against the floor beneath her. "I do not know. But it is not mine."

And that's what frustrates Renee now; despite everything, despite the countless murders of innocents

Nell has committed, despite the fact that she would have sacrificed countless more to a false god in a futile attempt to postpone something she believes is inevitable, she remains steadfast in her belief that she is not at fault. That there is a reason behind what she's doing. That everything she has ever done can be justified in the name of her cause.

"We are the same," Nell says, and Renee almost doesn't hear it, it's so quiet. Or maybe it's not, and everything else around them is just so loud. People's desperate pleas to be let out of the hall have died down, but the creaking and groaning of the ceiling above them has only gotten louder as the flames have gotten higher, roaring louder and louder with every growing second. The rain does nothing to douse the fire: It's spreading faster than the water can put it out

Nell holds out her hand towards Renee. It's soaked in her own blood, and her fingers are trembling, but the look in her one half-good eye is intent. Renee frowns at her and then looks down at her own hands. They, too, are covered in blood. Nell's, yes, but her own as well. Pablo's, too, and every other member of her community that she's ever had to stitch up. She clenches her fists together and looks back at Nell.

"We aren't," Renee shakes her head. "I am nothing like you. I would rather die than cause such mass destruction, than kill so many people. *Innocent* people. None of them ever deserved what they got. There's nothing after death, and you've been crazy the whole time."

"We are," Nell insists. "But I suppose there is no point in trying to convince you now." She chokes on her blood again and turns her head to the side to spit it out. It lands on the floor right by Renee's knees, and Renee fights the urge to move away from it. She doesn't know why. She's a medic, for fuck's sake. She's seen so much blood in her life that it's almost laughable to want to move away from it now. if she'd been a doctor before everything went to shit, she would have lost her licence here, trying to kill Nell. But she wasn't, and she never will be, because this really is the end of the world. She's sure of it. She doesn't know how she knows, but she's so certain that a pushing, burning ache pulses behind her eyes and in her temples. She thinks it might be Holly, that ache, trying to force her way back out and into control of her body. But Renee narrows her eyes against the pulsing, glares at Nell.

Something in the roof creaks again, and Renee looks back at Nell. This is it, then. This is how it ends. Here, on the surface, with someone she hates so thoroughly, so deeply in her bones, as her only company as it happens. Renee supposes she should be thankful she had as much time as she did, that she managed to extend her lifespan by two hundred years. But right here, right now, she's just tired. Ready. For it to all be over. For everything to end.

Ready to die.

She never thought she would be, but this has all gone on so long. She thinks she understands her predecessor's decision now. She wishes she didn't, wishes it had never come to this. But it has, and she does, and there's nothing she can do about it anymore. If the bunker really does survive this storm, Renee supposes she won't remember feeling any of this, and everything will just start over again. She hopes it doesn't, and then hates herself for thinking that because those people have become more family than coworkers over the last two hundred years.

"Just make it all stop," she whispers, and the only indication that Nell hears her is the slow blink she directs at Renee.

Then Nell says, "Lay down with me," and there is a tight pull in the back of Renee's brain, a desire to fight this. But she is helpless to Nell's suggestion as she follows the command. She lays her head right in the puddle of blood Nell threw up, but she can't bring herself to care.

CCXXXII

She stares up at the ceiling where it's crumbling to pieces, burning in places, and letting heavy droplets of rain litter the room.

It's almost peaceful, Renee thinks as she takes a deep breath and chokes on the smoke. Really, it is. If she can convince herself she's not about to die, lying here with Nell and looking up at the stars could be a peaceful, calm activity. Maybe if all that insanity were real, if Renee could believe it was real, she'd wonder if another world existed where she and Nell could lie like this, next to each other, watching the stars, and be happy.

But none of that's real, and none of this matters, and Renee's about to die because that sheet of ceiling above them is coming loose, and Nell's hated her this whole time, and—

ACKNOWLEDGEMENTS

The biggest thanks in the world, first of all, to my best friend Paige, for always being prepared to listen to me ramble on about a new book idea — including and especially this one as of late. I don't think I would have seriously considered this book in particular as 'publishable' if it weren't for you constantly telling me how much you love it and how hot you think Renee is despite her countless wrongs. Those hours upon hours of video calls where we would just sit and write in silence are some of my favourite we've had in the past year and a half.

Thanks also to the friends I met at uni; Amelie, Lilia, and Lily, for hyping me up in person, for indulging my rants about particular roadblocks I encountered while writing this book. Thank you for continuing to put up with my near-constant book-talk, whether it be something I'm reading or something I'm writing.

Additional thanks to my dog, Tessa, and my cat, Tilly, for always being a nuisance at the precise wrong times — aka, whenever I'm writing. You make writing feel more like a chore than something I enjoy when you're begging for food and attention at every waking hour of the day.

And finally, thank you to the four month summer break I had off between my first and second years of uni, where I managed to write and edit the entirety of this book. I may have felt delusional and sleep-deprived for the majority of that time, but I got it done. You were a real one.

Lou Parkes is a university student originally from Auckland, New Zealand, but is currently living and studying anthropology in Oxford. They have been telling and writing stories since their childhood, and have always told anyone who asks that they want to be an author when they grow up.

Twelve Weeks To Death is their first published work.

Website: louparkesauthor.com
Instagram: _loupark3s
TikTok: outoftheloup

Printed in Dunstable, United Kingdom